Invisible Bell

By

Julia Pelletier

J Pelletier

"Gryphon what's yours?"

Table of Contents

Chapter 1

Chapter 2

Chapter 3

Chapter 4

Chapter 5

Chapter 6

Chapter 7

Chapter 8

Chapter 9

Chapter 10

Chapter 11

Chapter 12

Chapter 13

Chapter 14

Chapter 15

Chapter 16

Chapter 17

Chapter 18

Chapter 19

Chapter 20

Chapter 21

Chapter 22

Chapter 23

Chapter 24

Chapter 25

Chapter 26

Chapter 27

©Copyright

Acknowledgement

© Copyright by Julia Pelletier 2017

This book is a work of fiction. All names, characters, locations and incidents are products of the author's imagination, or have been used fictitiously. Any resemblance to actual persons living or dead, locales, businesses or events is entirely coincident.

Licensing Notes:

This eBook is licensed for your personal enjoyment only. This eBook may not be re-sold or given away to other people. If you would like to share this book with another person, please purchase and additional copy for each recipient. If you're reading this book and did not purchase it, or it was not purchased for your use only, then please return to your eBook retailer and purchase your own copy. Thank you for respecting the hard work of this author.

The author of this work holds sole publishing rights. No part of this publication may be reproduced in whole or part, or stored in a retrieval system, or transmitted in any form or by any means, electronic, mechanical, photocopying, recording or otherwise without the permission of the rights holder. For information regarding permissions, email Julia Pelletier at: jpwritter02@gmail.com

Acknowledgement

I must start this with, if it wasn't for my husband I would never have had the courage to start; let alone finish this story. He has been my continued and strong driving force behind the telling of my tale for my debut novel, and for that I am truly thankful.

A massive thank you also goes to my editor Eve, for spending her valuable time on this labor of love.

Missie Jacks, my friend and fellow author, If I didn't have you to bounce ideas with this would have been a much longer process. So, thank you very much.

Trevor and Chelsea, without your help this would not be as beautiful as it is now.

To the handful of people who knew that this was happening I am truly grateful for your support and encouragement. There were countless moments of doubt, but with your kindness and honesty I was able to complete.

Chapter 1

She noticed him across the room. At first, it was just from scanning the café while she was looking up from her computer screen, but she was drawn to him due to his God-like appearance. No-one should be that striking! She needing to stop looking at him for her own sanity, so she continued with her perusal around the establishment as any kind of break was welcome at this point. Writing was her passion, but it took a lot of concentration and thought. She needed to pause. Her eyes were becoming strained from staring at the screen for a such long length of time.

While scanning the busy room, she saw a couple chatting, their conversation was just loud enough for her to hear,

"We can't do this here" said the female.

"Why not? No one is watching us, come on you know it will feel good." he said.

Looking over to them, Vicky was trying not to stare but she was caught up in what could possibly transpire right in front of her eyes. Sneaking a look beneath the table, Vicky saw his hand slip between his partners thighs under the helm of the almost non-existent piece of clothing, playfully joking.

"Stop! someone will see" she exclaimed with a giggle.

"No, they won't, and really does it matter? I love touching you: I can feel how much your body wants me to continue," he said it with such desire.

They indulged in gentle caresses and the occasional quick peck on the lips. Vicky's skin was beginning to warm, the

idea of that happening in front of her and in public was so naughty in a wonderful way. Vicky could feel her pulse begin to quicken. She wondered what it might feel like if it was her? Would she be more willing, or would she shut it down and wait until they were somewhere more private?

Pulling her eyes and ears from the frisky couple, her gaze followed the contours of the room. The sound of cups and plates touching, and the coffee that permeated the room was flirting with the senses: the aroma was intoxicating and very good at seducing the occupants of the bustling café.

There were groups of people in deep conversation. Snippets of discussions about, "What are you doing tomorrow?" and "Which movie should we go see?" could be heard above the dulcet tones of the patrons. The people in here were almost unaware of the waitress in her too-short dress refilling coffee or other refreshments. It was clear that the waitress knew it was a tad short and she was careful when picking up dropped items off the floor by bending at the knee rather than at the waist. Standing, she pulled at the helm of the dress and continued to the next table. That is where he was.

Their eyes met once the waitress carried onto the next table. His face showed no emotion but there was something about his eyes. Hypnotic, was the word. Smiling at him with the conventional greeting when caught in another's gaze, she tore her eyes away and continued to examine the room. However, just before returning to her work, she stole another glance at the man directly in front of her with the hypnotic eyes. Seeing he was watching her gave her a different feeling, a feeling of nervous excitement. He was handsome in the traditional sense. Dark hair – neat and short, but not too short, long enough to run fingers through. Clearly, he cared about his appearance; and those eyes kept drawing her in. She began feeling a little embarrassed as she was starting to fantasize about the texture and smell of his hair, how his skin felt on that strong face. She cleared her throat and decided to go back to work. Touching the screen to bring the words back up, she snuck one more look at the captivating man directly in front of her; who was no longer gazing in her direction, he was reading and seemed to be engrossed. With a quick shake of her head and a smile, she continued her writing. She did this every day here. The constant flow of people gave her inspiration and helped her when she was feeling blocked.

After two hours of work, she looked up to see the man with the hypnotic eyes gone. Maybe she dreamed him? Perhaps he was a figment of her imagination? Enjoying this thought, she decided to file that away in the "to play with" file in her head, knowing this could be a great fantasy. Feeling she had done enough work for the day, she packed up, paid her bill and said, "bye and see you tomorrow" to the staff and left.

The next day, Vicky was back in the café at the same table, doing the same thing, working on her writing. As she was totally absorbed in her work, she was unaware that he also had returned and was sitting in the exact same spot as the day before. When she took her break, she began to look around the room again. Vicky Loved being amongst the hub-bub of the café, this is where Vicky

3

felt not so alone. She could write to her heart's content and at least being in this venue she was surrounded by people, even if she was not part of any conversation. It was also a wonderful place to gather inspiration for whichever story she was writing at this time. Situated where she was within the establishment allowed for her to watch the people outside passing by; as well as seeing the patrons within the restaurant. With a quick intake of air, she parted her lips and gasped. He was there again. This time his face was different: a little smile danced at one corner of his mouth. It was a wicked little grin.

She looked up meeting his eyes and saw they were smiling back at her. Nothing else seemed to matter at that moment. Her concentration on her work was gone. She had the desire to kiss the smile on his lips, touch his face and smell his hair. She was not entirely sure what to do as she knew she could never be bold enough to approach him. Instead, she busied herself with her lap top. However, every few moments, she would look up and be caught in the web that was him. As a moth to flame, she was to him. Looking at him gave her body warmth she had not felt before. No, she was no virgin and in touch with herself, but this was something different. It also didn't help that he just stared back, not saying anything and made no advances too.

Pretending to be busy seemed to be the only solution but she knew fine well that her mood and concentration had taken a turn. There was no way she could go back to work today. Looking around again, she was unable to stop herself from gravitating to where he was sitting. Only he was gone. Avidly looking for him, she couldn't find him. Her pulse was racing, and her breath was heavy. She closed her eyes in attempt to calm down but abruptly opened them as the sound of someone at her table gave her hope that it was him. It wasn't. In fact, it was the waitress from the other day. Her name tag said "Daisy"; however, there really was no way of knowing if that really was her name or just a tag that was left over from an old employee. Vicky looked up at the waitress, who was holding a glass of ice water.

"This was sent over to you by someone."

Vicky was confused. She didn't know anyone on a personal level in here, so she asked who sent it.

Daisy just shrugged her shoulders and said, "I'm just doing my job, drink it or don't. It's up to you." and with that, she sashayed away.

Looking around again to see if anyone looked like they were looking at her, Vicky didn't see anyone. The ice water was refreshing and cool going down her throat. It was strangely satisfying. Who would have thought water was able to do that?

Vicky finished the glass of water, packed up and left for the day. On her way out, her mind drifted back to the man with the eyes. What would it be like to talk to him? What would his voice sound like? As she was totally distracted with her private questions, she was completely oblivious to what was before her out on the pavement. Because of this, she was not aware of him leaning against a car.

"Done so soon?"

Vicky heard a voice, looked up and at that same moment dropped her bag. It was him! She wasn't sure who he was talking to, so she bent down to retrieve the bag that she had dropped. Again, she heard his voice.

"Did the water help?" Vicky's eyes stared at the ground. Was he talking to her? How did he know about the water? Surely lots of people were drinking water in a café? Most people had it to accompany their meal. Deciding that he was not talking to her, Vicky retrieved the bag she had dropped and stood up tall to readjust the strap when that voice spoke again. "I sure hope that that bag has some serious protection in it. As, from experience, a dropped laptop does not do so well."

He was totally talking to her. Vicky was dumfounded. No one talked to her: she was invisible. Always had been and figured she would always be. Even in school, a nice private school, where the who's who of the business world sent their children, Vicky just sort of blended into the walls. Not that she was a wall flower, she just didn't feel the need to be the most popular or become part of a particular social group. Vicky kept her head down and achieved what she wanted out of school, went onto University, got her degree in business and

was now living the life she wanted. Yes, she could very well go and work for her father; however, that was not what she wanted to do. "Excuse me, it is customary to acknowledge someone once they have started a conversation with you. A simply hello would suffice."

Feeling like a deer in headlights, Vicky stared at the man with the amazing eyes. Struggling for words was not normally an issue for her but this man – this God – was causing her to not find her voice.

His voice was like molten lava, hot and vibrant. And like lava, it had the ability to stop her completely in her tracks.

"Um me... you are talking to me?" Vicky said, hoping it didn't sound as pathetic as she thought it did.

"Yes, I am talking to you. Whom else would I ask about ice water or a dropped lap top? I don't see anyone else dropping one."

He was still leaning against the car looking relaxed but there was something there, something that resembled power. Vicky shifted on her feet. This man made her nervous, basically because she wanted him in the worst way. Growing up Vicky was taught etiquette and how to behave in polite society so did eventually respond.

"Well, as we haven't really been introduced, and you just started a conversation that I was not aware of, how was I too know it was me that you were talking too? Regardless of that, hello."

Having said her piece, she put her rather shaky hand out to him. It was out there waiting for him to take it which felt like an eternity. She so desperately wanted him to. Then she would know what his skin felt like.

He tilted his head to one side, looked at her hand then her face, smiled and said, "Hello."

With that, he lent forward to come off the car. Vicky was so sure he was going to take her hand but instead he turned around and opened the back door of the car and got in. All Vicky saw was herself in the reflection of the window, staring back. She felt like a chump. To make matters worse, her hand was still out hanging in the air.

Someone coming down the sidewalk slapped it as they passed in front of her and said, "High five!"

He at least touched her, but the sting sizzled in her opened palm. It was not the man she wanted to touch her, but it was something. While she was looking at the man sauntering down the sidewalk, the car "the man with the eyes" was in drove away. When she looked again at it, it was gone. Feeling ridiculous, she walked the short five minutes to her house. On the way there, she told herself that tomorrow was another day and she didn't know anyone who would pass comment on what just happened. He probably wouldn't be there anyway. Why would he? He clearly had tons of money and was just having a break during his work day, so she surmised. There was no way he would be there tomorrow, right?

Chapter 2

The following day, there she was back in the café at the same table, doing the same thing: writing, and it was going well. The story she was writing was flowing from her brain and was practically writing itself.

When Vicky had arrived, she looked for the man that had caused her to toss and turn and not get any sleep. Her mind was on overdrive all night long until the wee hours of the morning when she finally decided to locate the "to play with" file and made up the best fantasy she could think of. Her experience with sex was not vast but she had always been able to bring herself to orgasm with her imagination and touch. She knew that there were certain parts of her body that were more sensitive than others.

Vicky's actual experience with sex was lacking, and when she'd had sex, which was at University, it was not great, nothing to talk about. Her ex, Mike, thought it was fantastic. He had loved the fact that she was a virgin. He called her his "pure China doll". Ugh, it had made her skin crawl. The actual act was a case of her lying on her back and him doing a lot of grunting and groaning. He had lifted her tank top to above her breasts and he took off her pajama shorts. Vicky had heard of foreplay, but Mike didn't believe in it. He had said that it was for people who were not into each other and so therefore need it to get into the mood. He had told her to lay back on the bed with her legs open. She was so embarrassed: all the lights where on and he could see everything as could she. Mike pulled his penis out of his shorts and was licking his lips while stroking his hand up and down his shaft. Too afraid to move, Vicky looked up at the ceiling and hoped that his member would fit. The biology of the act she knew but it baffled her how it actually would.

Mike rolled a condom onto his penis and brought it to her opening. It was an odd sensation; it was so hard and hot. It surprised her. The next thing she knew, he pushed inside of her with a strong thrust. She screamed out as something popped inside. Instant pain happened.

Mike said that was normal and kept going. Tears streamed down her cheeks, he thought this was in enjoyment. It wasn't; but she refused to give up. She had heard the girls in class and the locker-room talk about how fabulous sex was and what it had felt like, so she wanted to feel that sensation. It never happened.

He groped her breast like he was turning the knob on a radio and grunted twice loudly then lay on top of her body. That was it! He pulled himself out of her, making her wince. He said how fantastic that was and how he had never felt that way before with anyone, how he felt so special that she had entrusted him with her virginity. Vicky really thought it was wasted on him and, if she could have, she would have taken it back. She was really sore and couldn't wait for him to leave so she could have a soak in the bath.

Not because of the sex, Vicky had ended their relationship shortly after that, blaming her need to study. For the rest of the time at University, she didn't bother with men. If she felt the need to have an orgasm, she gave it to herself. Now that she knew what worked for her, it didn't take long for the desired effect to take place.

With that in mind, Vicky's fantasy about the man with the eyes (she didn't know his name and couldn't figure a name that would suit him) began on the sand. She was lying sunbathing and he was coming out of the water. She had used this one before many times but never had a face to go with the body. The sun was at its peak and therefore it was so hot on the sand. Thankfully, she had brought a large mat so that she was not directly on the sand, even though she was lying on a towel. A double layer of protection was never a bad thing against the baking sand. Just walking on it was enough to burn the instep of your foot. All of a sudden, there was a shadow above her. Opening her eyes and squinting, she could make out a form. A male form. Bringing her hand up to shade her eyes allowed her to open them further. In doing so, she saw what she thought was a Greek God standing, dripping glacier water on her stomach. The instant it landed on her skin it sizzled and evaporated: the sudden chill was both shocking and welcomed in this heat. Without talking, he bent down and lifted her up in his arms. The connection of their skin gave relief to her heated skin. She tried to protest but it was useless. The feeling was bliss. He stopped any conversation with his lips, tightly fusing their mouths together.

Pulling away to gather air into her lungs, she allowed herself to look at his face. He truly was God like; so perfectly chiseled and masculine, with defined cheek bones that begged to be touched. Without thinking, that is what she did, catching drops of water on her finger and feeling them cascade down to her hand. The sensation was so gentle it could have been ticklish if it was not so erotic. He was no longer looking at her but straight ahead with a determined expression. He clearly was focused on where they were going.

Vicky opened her mouth to ask what was happening when he again sealed their lips together. Realizing that he meant for her not speak, she nestled into his shoulder. He smelled of the ocean. Without thinking, she licked him. Her tongue darted out and caught another drop of water. So salty and warm. And all the while, he continued his path to his desired destination. She moaned in her head or at least she thought she had. His chest was strong and, like the rest of him, well defined. To say that he was comfortable to lie on would not be correct, he was a mass of pure muscle and the strength of his strides across the sand were steady and purposeful. On the occasion, he did look at Vicky, he just smiled.

She turned to look where they were going. She could see that what lay ahead was a gathering of trees and what seemed to be a tent under them, with flowing layers of billowing white material that would caress the sand along with the steady breeze. Upon arriving at the tent, Vicky took this opportunity to look up. She could see the leaves on the palm trees gently swaying with the wind, doing a beautiful dance and providing a melody that was hypnotic. Looking over his shoulder, she could no longer see any of the other people that were on the beach. I was only them in this oasis. He ever-so gently put her down until her feet touched the sand. Unlike out on the beach, this sand was cool and refreshing on the soles of her feet and was almost cold in comparison. She also realized that her body was damp and, with the breeze, a tad too cool.

Her skin had goose bumps and her nipples were erect under her bikini top: they were straining to escape

12

the confines of the cloth. The white bikini that had complemented her tanned skin was now see-through. She never swam in this suit but, as it was tiny, it allowed for the most sun exposure without too many tan lines. The top was so small that it barely covered her breasts, just enough of a triangle to do the job. The bottoms hung low on her hips with a single strap attaching the sides together. The back cut up her bottom in a wide V so not to be a G-string but providing a little coverage of her cheeks so as to not be indecent.

He grabbed her hand and led her to the table that was in the center of the tent. She was happy to oblige and do as he pleased. He picked her up and placed her on the table and slid her legs apart. The cool breeze lifted her hair and brushed it against her back. The caress excited her, and her breath hitched. His hands started a journey up the inside of her legs; barely touching her, skimming the cool skin. The goosebumps rose, following the trail of his fingers. He had reached the white triangle of her bottoms and brought his hands up the front of her most private of areas. She could feel that dampness was beginning to pool between her most sensitive lips.

Hoping he would delve into the wetness, she closed her eyes and laid her head back. Her hands grasped the edge of the table and she gave herself to him as an offering. She was willing him to take her but, instead, he continued with his journey up the sides of her ribcage to the underside of her breasts. They had swollen and her nipples where taut. With each breath, they rubbed against the fabric of her top, creating heightened pleasure.

His fingers were running up the center of her chest, teasing her with the touch. Not able to stand it anymore, she let out a frustrated moan and he was on her. His mouth was devouring her. Their lips joined, and he forced his tongue into her mouth. She accepted with greed and

was lost in the ecstasy that was the kiss. Bringing her hands up, she ran them up his strong muscular back and, once reaching his shoulders, brought him to her so their bodies were in contact. His cool skin from the ocean water was soon replaced with heat.

While the passion was being consumed in the kiss, his hands had so deftly undone the back of her top. It was only being held up with the weight of their bodies. He moved his torso, allowing it to fall into her lap. She was not aware that this had happened as she was lost in the swirl of sensations surrounding her. His hands went to her face and cradled it with the strength of a warrior but the gentleness of a lover. He pierced his fingers through her hair and pulled her head back. This separated their lips and her mouth gaped with the angle. His mouth consumed her left nipple. Instant pleasure shot through her body, making her buck a little which pulled her bottoms tight against her cleft. The pressure was intense, and she knew she wouldn't be able to contain herself for long.

He had moved his mouth to the other breast and was doing a dance with his tongue, teasing around the nipple with little flickers of touch. She was unable to stay quiet. She moaned. This fueled his attempt to devour her nipple. With his teeth, he gently racked them over, tugging at the tip, which sent shock waves through her body until they culminated at the center of her. His other hand, that had been bracing her back, was now cupping her other breast, rolling her nipple between his thumb and forefinger, gently pulling to elongate it.

The breeze was washing them with light touches. The sensation was building up within her and was almost peaking. He removed his hand and mouth from her breasts. He brought his mouth back to hers and speared his tongue into her mouth. His hand pressed her mound and stars exploded in her head. She could hardly breathe as the orgasm took over her body and she came apart. She stiffened, then sagged against him. Pulling her mouth away from his, she gasped for air.

Vicky herself was gasping and exhausted. She stretched out her limbs across her bed. Thanking every day for buying the king size bed, she was sated and hot. When had the temperature risen in her room? With the press of a button, she was able to activate the overhead fan and the blades came to life, circulating the air and wrapping her in the cool flow. Rolling over, she slept but not deeply: she was still thinking about him and this was causing a problem that she would figure out later.

Chapter 3

Not finding him sitting anywhere around her; and realizing she was just daydreaming about her wonderful orgasm, Victoria decided that she needed to stop procrastinating and get focused on the job at hand. She really needed to get this project wrapped up. One day she might consider publishing her books but for now she just liked writing and then going back to them in her own time.

She was so immersed in what she was doing, she didn't hear anyone approaching nor did she hear anyone sit down at the table she was at. What she did hear was someone clearing their throat. It didn't occur to her it was anything more than that, so she continued with what she was doing. "You really do not pick up on social cues, do you?"

It was him. She froze, her fingers where resting on the keys of her laptop. Bringing her eyes up over the top of the screen, she could see him. He was sitting at her table with his hands folded on the table top. He was staring at her again. She had to respond but all she could think about was the most amazing fantasy she had enjoyed about him the night before. How do you talk to someone you did that with, without their knowledge? "Uh hello," she said tentatively.

A flush was creeping into her cheeks; he loved watching her and had done so for quite some time. She had only seen him two days in a row, but he had noticed her the first time he had entered the café, which was at least six months ago. In fact, much to his chagrin, he was captivated by her and had asked himself the question of would she do? Of course she would, but how did he broach the subject? He had done the usual things he did when picking the latest one. However, this girl was different.

As with the others, he had done a background check of her and her family but, unlike the others, she didn't see it. She didn't see what happened when she entered a room or the café every day. She didn't see the same faces watching her, struggling to find the words to initiate conversation with her. It was not just the men or the wait staff, it was also the curious girls who were captivated by her. When she walked by, most would moisten their lips and the men readjusted their member. It was so erotic to see so many affected by her and her oblivious to it. He knew that she would be the most exquisite one yet; he had to have her. If the color that was entering her face was anything to go by, he knew that what he could do to and with her body was more than he could contain. None of the others had wanted to shake his hand, they all knew about him and what he did. There was a waiting list a mile long to be taken by him. But Vicky was different in so many ways. She didn't know who he was or what he did professionally or privately. That was one of the things that drew him to her.

Regarding her with his steady eyes, he had ascertained that she would be exceptional. Even watching her across the table, he knew it was now or never... and never was not an option. The wording had to be just so for her to be interested and that was his specialty. Words and closing the deal had made him extremely wealthy, which had allowed him to cultivate his pleasures and desires. Essentially, he now worked to allow him the time it took for his pleasure: this had become his passion. He loved working and he excelled in the boardroom, but he loved his "playtime" more. These days he was able to have the time he wanted. And he knew that he had to have Victoria. Yes, everyone else called her Vicky but to him she was Victoria, regal and beautiful.

Her greeting was meek, but he was quite sure that there was power behind that gentle little voice. He smiled and was confident he would bring it to the surface on many occasions.

"Ah, I am so glad that you are responding to me today. I was beginning to worry that you truly lived in a bubble which contained you and your laptop. It must be very important as for hours upon hours you spend staring and ferociously typing. Would you care to share the mystery of what it is you are doing?"

Vicky still couldn't believe that he was talking to her, actually having a conversation with him. He had asked a question but for the life of her she couldn't remember what it was. She was in shock and just was staring at him. Looking around, she could see men and women gazing at her. They looked disappointed. Obviously, they wanted his attention so why was he here sitting across from her?

"What are you writing?" He asked again with more authority.

It was enough to bring her attention back to him. She jumped and said, "Um, it's just a book I have been working on, nothing special."

"Well, what is it about, how long have you been writing it?"

"Um, I have been writing it for about a year. I keep writing it then when I read it I don't like what I have read. So, I start again. It really doesn't matter anyway as I only do this for me." She sounded so sad and certain of the fact that it was only for her, little did she know that many people had read her previous work and were enthralled with her as an author.

He himself had read all of her work, of which there was many. It is amazing how easy you can access information if you know how and where to look. Victoria didn't bother with putting it under password protection so hacking into her computer was not difficult at all. He had found what he wanted to within one hour of her leaving the café that first day six months ago and systematically read every word she had written. In all, she had written seven books ranging in subject but always with such poetry that you were caught up in each word and had to know what happened next. "Oh, but that would be tragic. I've seen you work tirelessly for a while now and for no one to read your work would be a shame. Please allow me the pleasure of being privy to your work."

"No, I don't think so but thank you for the offer. Hang on, what do you mean you have been watching me for a while?" she just realized what he had said and was taken aback. "Like I just said, I've been watching you for a while and you were in such concentration about your task, you were unaware of the world around you. I too have that ability, but it is not within the realm of writing but something else that I am very passionate about." His eyes lit up when saying the last part. There was something there, Vicky was unsure what it was but had feeling she was likely to find out.

"Okay, well let me introduce myself. My name is Damion... and you are?"

That had surprised him, he never told the women his first name: it was always Mr. Foster. This was a first, and quite exciting. All she had to do was just say yes when the time was right.

So that was his name, Damion. She would never have thought that to be his name, but it suited him perfectly. Now she had a face and a name to her mystery fantasy man. Oh, that's right, she'd had a fantasy about him. The color was coming back to her face again.

"And your name is...?"

"Oh sorry, Vicky. Well, it's Victoria but no one calls me that unless I am in trouble." She said with an innocent smile.

"Victoria. That is a beautiful name. Suits you to a tee. I shall call you Victoria."

It was a statement, not a question. Normally, she didn't like people calling her that but the way he said it made her shiver. If that was the reaction that his voice had on her then what would have happened if he touched her? She was ready to find out but didn't want to seem too eager; that would just be desperate. She was, but didn't want to give off that impression to Damion. Just saying his name in her mind caused goose bumps to form along her arms. Unconsciously rubbing her hands along them to remove the chill, she wished she had brought a light jacket. She rarely felt the cold down here in Florida as she was a northern girl and knew what cold meant. This was some other kind of chill that she couldn't quite place.

Watching her, he saw the color creep back into her face and loved it. But he wanted to know what made her do that. Also, the statement about her name gave him one of the answers he needed. That was she responded extremely well to his command. The time had come to ask even though they had just met. It had to be done now.

"I am going to ask you a question and I expect you to answer immediately, if you would be so kind," he finished off with a gentle compromise to not seem too dominant. It would not do to scare her off before she even knew what was coming next.

"Okay, what is your question?" she asked quietly, ever hopeful that he wanted to see her outside of the café.

"All I need is seven days of your life. Do you think this could be a possibility? Can you stop writing for that long? If so, then I promise you that you won't regret it. I am aware that you and I have just met, but just give me your gut reaction: what do you think?"

Chapter 4

That is not what Victoria thought Damion would ask: what does he mean seven days? What will happen in those days? She had just met him, and she did want to be with him but was this too much, was she able to be that bold? It was just one week of her life, but she had never been a risk taker. Looking around, Vicky felt it was as if the café was waiting for her response. Surely no one had actually heard what he had asked her. What if they had? Would it be foolish to give in to the yearning desire to be with him or was it truly not safe? Taking a deep breath and letting it out slowly, she decided then and there: why not? She could do this. It wasn't like anyone was going to check up on her as her family lived in New York and didn't expect to hear from her for a couple of weeks. She didn't have a job but had enough money to sustain her lifestyle; her father had made sure of that. Her entire family knew that she was a writer they were just waiting for her to tell them openly.

The house she loved and lived in was her parents; they had called it their vacation home but never used it. When they came down, they stayed in hotels, saying the amenities were at their fingertips and all they had to do was call and it arrived, whatever the service they requested. So she really was on her own, she liked it that way. She had space and could do what she wanted when she wanted to. The only thing she was strict about was coming to the café and writing for at least four hours a day. Yes, she could do it at home, but the stimulation was not there. So why not take a leap of faith she never did anything risky or exciting and this would definitely be both. Taking a deep breath, she once more opened her mouth and gave her answer.

"Yes, why not? I can take a week's vacation from my day-to-day living. What are we doing?" Looking wide eyed and vulnerable, she waited for his explanation to what the week would entail.

Pleased that his gamble had paid off, Damion smile was so substantial it lit the room up. His entire face was smiling: now he just had to plan what he was going to do first. Well, not first, that was always the same, but after that. With Victoria, he didn't want to do the usual, he wanted something more. Something that was exceptional. First things first, he had to make the arrangements for her to get to the house. That was not going to be difficult but keeping it a secret was going to be interesting.

"Great! Right, I shall have the car pick you up from your home tomorrow morning at seven sharp. What is your address? As you walk here every day, I'm sure it is not too far. Then it shall start. Pack a light bag; you will not need much. I very much look forward to seeing you soon."

With that he got up and left without a backward glance at her. She sat stunned. What had she just done? She couldn't nor wouldn't back out now, but he had simply left the café with instructions. He had asked for her address but left before she could give them to him. So how was he going to be at her home? Feeling very confused, Vicky decided to leave for the day. Going home and have nice hot soak in the bathtub sounded like heaven right now, especially after her experience with Damion.

Chapter 5

It was a fretful night as Vicky tossed and turned. In fact, since she had seen Damion, she had not slept well at all. As sleep evaded her, she was up sipping coffee at five in the morning, staring out of the window and waiting for the sun to make its daily appearance. It was very dark, not just because it was before the sunrise but the dark that was ominous, foreboding. It gave the sense that nothing good would come from this day. Or maybe that was just how she felt.

As the sun did make its appearance, the clouds hung low keeping the sun trapped from view, which meant that there was a storm brewing. It was going to be a fantastic storm that would have lightning dancing across the sky and thunder shaking the ground. Looking out of the window and sipping her coffee, Vicky was able to watch the dark grey clouds roll closer to her house. The change in color was subtle at first then became strikingly obvious. The grey clouds were swallowing the lighter, fluffier clouds that stood in their way. There was no warning when the rain started: it was torrential. Pounding the ground with such force, raindrops were bouncing up and attacking the windows.

Vicky was so lost in the display of the storm that she did not hear anyone approach her front door. In fact, she didn't hear anything but the sound of the storm, lulling her into a hypnotic state. Had she been paying attention, she would have noticed a car pulling up and sitting outside of her house. She would have also noticed that the same car had been sitting in front of her house for the last six months. And, she would have noticed that attached to the car was a camera that had allowed Damion to view her at all times from any location he happened to be at.

Damion had set up a screen that gave him the ability to view Vicky at any time or place while he was around the world. He didn't invade her house, which he usually did to the women the house. Not knowing what to do she looked around and, as she had already agreed to do this, she took a deep breath and followed P. out of the house. In the last minute, she grabbed her handbag off of the front table, locked the door and headed towards the vehicle at the curb.

The rain was still assaulting the ground and in turn the drops ricocheted off the ground pelted Vicky and P. The mad dash to the car was quick but not fast enough to stop getting soaked. By the time P. had opened the door, it was clear that she was soaked through and in need of a change of clothes. Unfortunately, that was not to be as her luggage, small as it was, was in the trunk of the car and not within her reach.

P. calmly walked to the driver's door and got in. He started the car and, as soon as he did, the cold air-conditioning blasted her making her colder, if that was possible, than before. It brought goose bumps to her skin and her nipples were so erect they were fighting the confinements of her white T-shirt. While wringing out her hair onto the floor, Vicky tried to shift the air away from her body and directed it up to the ceiling. P. casually handed a towel to her from the front and pulled away from the curb.

"Thank you for the towel, can you believe the storm?" Vicky was trying, badly, to make small talk. However, P. was having none of it. He ignored her and continued driving. He despised small talk and wouldn't engage in the act. Instead, he focused on driving to the private airstrip that would then take them to the house.

It really wasn't a house it was more like a fort from medieval times. Very gothic and vast, with gardens surrounding it and, to make it even more authentic, it even had a moat surrounding the perimeter. Damion took his security very seriously and did not scrimp on any of it, especially where he "played". Perhaps more than his main office, the fort had many more things that needed to be kept safe and private.

Realizing that talking to P. was futile, Vicky continued to dry herself off as much as possible. Looking out of the window seemed to be pointless as due to the storm it was dark and gloomy. The scenery was what you would expect of Florida, palm trees lined the roads and the grass was green; other than that, nothing really recognizable was to be seen. She knew she was not beach side anymore but other than that she didn't know where she was or where she was going. Instead she sat back, towel dried her hair and closed her eyes. She had agreed to this so for one week wherever they were going was up to Damion. The sound of rain was soothing and, as she was wound up with not knowing anything, listening to the rain was relaxing and took her mind off the unknown.

It was not long before they had arrived at their destination. P. pulled up to the gate and, like magic, the gates swung open. Feeling that they had stopped, Vicky opened her eyes to see a landing strip before her. Clearly, they had arrived at an airport of some kind; it was not big enough for commercial airplanes, but it was definitely an airport all the same. Vicky was beginning to feel somewhat excited. Even though she had no idea where she was going, it was on an airplane and that meant going somewhere different. She loved flying; her family would travel on vacation all the time so flying meant an adventure and this definitely was one.

Once through the security gates, P. drove them to a large hanger on the left of the gate. Vicky could make out the name above the hanger doors. In big back letters, it said Foster Holdings Inc. Not knowing what or who that was, she figured it was a company but hadn't heard of it before. Inside the hanger doors was a beautiful G6 jet, sleek and magnificent. Surely, she was not going to be on that! She had only ever traveled on commercial planes, to go on private was both scary and exciting.

P. pulled the car alongside the plane and Vicky could see that the door was open and the steps where down. Just as the car stopped, a man appeared at the door and was making his way down the steps. P. opened her door and she was momentarily stuck. P. just waited patiently for her to exit the car.

He could tell she was nervous; in fact, he knew she was the moment she had opened her door at the house. The whole way to the airport he could hear her taking deep breaths clearly to calm herself. He had no idea if it had worked or not, but it really didn't matter, they were all the same. All the women that he brought to Damion were nervous. They pretended to be ready for anything, they even knew what to expect, well they kind of did, not one really knew until they were at the house. Once there, they either put on a brave face or they fled back to where they had come from.

That is why the screening process was so rigorous (until Damion had found Victoria, she was the same but different). P. had never seen Damion look at any of the women, of which there were many, the way he looked at Victoria. He had even told her his given name – that was a rule he had never broken before, so therefore she must mean something different to him. She must mean more to him than a toy to play with and discard once he had his fill.

P. had never felt that way for a woman before nor did he think he ever would. After what he had seen at the house, it had changed his opinion of the fairer species. He tried to stay completely impartial to the wants and needs of his boss but sometimes it was too much to bear. Not the act of playing but the willingness of the women and the degradation they appeared to enjoy. How they could endure and enjoy that? That was beyond his comprehension. Not that it mattered to him one way or another. This was Damion's thing and not his. All he had to do was his job and, at the moment, it was to make sure Victoria got on the plane and he drove her to the house. Then it was up to the staff there until he was called on again to take her home.

Vicky readied herself and left the safety of the car. Walking the short distance to the steps of the plane seemed like a mile. Concentrating on the ground seemed to be a better way to calm her nerves but, once she glanced up, she could see the man from the airplane looking at her. He had kind eyes, a warm smile and looked non-threating. He was just waiting for her to do something. What, she was not sure. His smile broadened and he said,

"Hello, Victoria, it is nice to meet you. My name is Charles and I will be your Capitan for this flight. The flight itself will be good and, once we are out of this current location, the weather is clear. No need to worry about the storm, we shall be far above it in no time."

Any fears she had about the weather, which she really didn't even think about, were gone in a flash. Charles could have told her the worst news and she would have felt at ease. It was an odd feeling to look at someone and be at total peace. Unlike with Damion: when she looked at him, a fire burned inside of her. She felt a yearning for contact, skin on skin, but was unsure if that would be enough to sate her desires. Her face flushed and her breath hitched, just thinking about Damion had a huge impact on her body as well as her mental state. Not trusting herself to speak, she nodded slightly and made her way up the steps. Charles followed her, and P. brought up the rear with her luggage in tow.

Vicky thought she was going to need to duck and squeeze down the aisle, however, the inside of the plane was rather large. It was very deceptive from the outside. Once inside, she was able to stand straight and there was still room above her head. On either side of the aisle were plush white leather seats and walnut wooden tables. It was rather attractive with the wood and the white – the contrast was pleasing to the eye. Clearly, this was an office in the sky. Whoever this plane belonged to was a very busy man and needed to have a mobile office. Once seated, Vicky realized just how comfortable the seats were. The leather was soft and cradled her body. P. had also taken his seat somewhere behind her. She didn't want to look so she stared out of the window. A stewardess in a white blouse and black pencil skirt came towards Vicky. She had no idea where she had come from and didn't remember seeing her when embarking the plane.

"Would you care for a light refreshment? Perhaps some champagne and strawberries?"

"No thank you. It is too early for champagne, but I will have some strawberries and a glass of water if I may?"

The stewardess smiled and proceeded to the back of the aircraft, presumably where the galley would be. Vicky did start to ponder where they were going and how long it would take to get there. Finally, she plucked up the courage and looked around only to find P. looking at her. Catching his eye, she smiled and cleared her throat to start to ask what their final location was when he got up and walked up to the cockpit. After that, Vicky gave up trying to talk to him. It was obvious that he had no regard for her at all. The stewardess came back with the water and strawberries and placed them on the table.

"Please fasten your seat belt as we are ready for departure," came over the intercom from the pilot. So, there were some similarities with commercial and private planes, and safety was one of them. Looking frantically for the seat belt, Vicky was about to call for P. when the stewardess reached down the sides of her and pulled the seatbelt from within the chair. Vicky was surprised at how intimate that felt, the warmth on her skin from being grazed by the stewardess. Now that she was right in front of her, Vicky was able to read her name tag "Sally"; however, this time she was sure that this was her name unlike the waitress in the café.

Without even looking at Vicky, P. walked straight back to his seat and buckled in. He knew the ritual of take-

30

off and landing it was his favorite part. In his life, he had spent most of it on and out of a plane. He never divulged what he had done before working for Damion to anyone but Damion, but P.'s knowledge of things was vast. He also knew that the flight was going to take between two and two and half hours to their destination. He had no intention of let Vicky know this though, that was not part of his job. His job was to make sure she arrived safely and that he had almost accomplished. He laid his head back and decided to sleep. His morning had started very early or he had a very late night depending on how you looked at it. Either way, he was ready for some sleep. At least he would have some down time soon and that he was very much looking forward too. With a grin on his face, he closed his eyes and fell into a dreamless sleep.

Vicky had hoped that she would get some answers from someone about the whereabouts they were going but it seemed that, if possible, people avoided her. Now that she was securely fastened in and happily munching on strawberries, which were succulent and bursting with flavor, she sort of wished she had accepted the champagne instead of water. However, she just couldn't bring herself to drink alcohol that early in the morning. No matter what she felt, drinking before twelve was hard for her to do. Unless you were having mimosas with brunch, that was acceptable.

Once she had finished her snack, Victoria knew that the only way she was going to get through this flight and not trying to talk to anyone was by sleeping. The hum of the jets was surprisingly relaxing, and she was very tired having not slept well last night anticipating today's festivities. She closed her eyes and drifted into a dead sleep.

31

P. grabbed hold of Victoria's shoulder and gave her a shake. She looked very peaceful but it was time to go. The plane had landed and there was a car waiting for them to take them the rest of the journey.

Vicky woke with a bit of a start. Her body was shaking and getting her eyes to open was a bit of a problem as they didn't want to open. Once they did, the first thing that Vicky saw was P. He was leaning down in front of her speaking to her but she had no idea what he was saying. She had slept harder than she thought so coming too was a little fuzzy.

"We are here, it's time to go," P. said with no emotion at all.

"Where are we going? Oh, that's right you don't talk to me, do you? Is that part of your orders?" Vicky said sarcastically, hoping to get some kind of response. She knew that he wouldn't say anything but at least she had tried.

Stretching her arms above her head, she yawned and looked out of the window, however there was nothing to see as the plane was in a hanger. In fact, it looked exactly like the one they had driven to earlier but the only difference was the plane was not facing the doors but rather the back of the hanger. P. was still standing in front of her waiting for her to move. She looked at him and let out a big sigh and unbuckled her seat belt and got up. She stood still for a few seconds to stretch and regain her surroundings then she started following P. out of the plane.

Using her hand, she combed her hair, just knowing that she didn't look her best. That had started with the downpour this morning and not having any time to do something with her hair. Finally, she gave up on combing it and pulled a hair tie off of her left wrist and tugged her hair into a high pony tail. Her clothes had dried so she felt a bit more human, so to speak. As she was climbing down the stairs, she noticed – or rather her skin had noticed – that it was chilly, not cold, but not the searing heat that took your breath away in Florida. They definitely where not in Florida anymore but she truly had no idea where she was. Scanning the outside of the plane didn't help either as the doors to the hanger where closed and there was a black car waiting as P. had said.

Victoria's skin was chilled and she really wished she had a cardigan or a light jacket at that moment. At least she had the foresight to wear jeans and boat shoes so her bottom half was warm, now she had to figure out how to warm the top half. In her suitcase, she had a light jacket but as she had no idea where that was. She just hugged herself and made her way over to the car – well, it wasn't just a car, it was a stretch limousine. P. had opened the door when she heard someone call out her name. She looked around to see Charles, the pilot, smiling and waving at her.

"Look forward to seeing you again Victoria," he said standing in the doorway of the plane.

She was about to say something but decided against it as what do you say? She had no idea where she was or what she was going to be doing. She had essentially given her life away to someone else for a week. Of course, she would not do anything that she didn't like. She was strong enough to stand her ground and didn't actually believe that Damion would put her in that situation, or she had hoped that was the case as she really knew nothing about him either. This was a huge leap of faith for her but she was drawn to him in a way that she had never felt before. So, in the end, it didn't matter anyway, she had to see him again. Vicky smiled back at Charles and got into the limousine. Once seated, she put her head back and closed her eyes briefly. The door closed and she looked up. P. was sitting in the driver's seat again so she knew they were going somewhere else.

"There is a blanket to the right of you if you are still cold," P. said. It was more of a statement than a suggestion.

Looking to her right, she felt rather than saw the blanket. It was soft and thick, the kind you would have on the back of a couch in a lodge in the mountains. She tried to see the color scheme but it was too dark inside the car figuring that once they were out of the hanger she could see it; she just draped it over her body and snuggled into the seat.

The next thing she knew was the car was moving. Vicky was looking forward to being able to see outside so she could get an idea of where they were. As in where in the world they were! She knew they were not in the United States as she did not need her passport, but as she had slept and no one had told her how long she had been out, she figured that it was around lunch time as her stomach gave a sound of need for food. She tried to look out of the window as she heard what sounded like a garage door opening but she could not see anything to her left or right and when she looked at the wind screen, her view was blocked by a partition. This was frustrating; she couldn't see anything but she could at least stretch out. She started talking to P. hoping that he could hear her.

"Why does the tint have to be so dark? I mean, does the person that owns this car feel that threatened? The glass is probably bullet proof. They are either really well known, like a celebrity or they are really paranoid!"

P. did not answer any of her questions, he just said,

"It will not take that long to get to the destination."

"Wow, you really have a way with words." She said, sarcastically.

Obviously, she was not going to get any information out of P. She had tried and failed so sat back and pondered and stewed about this odd scenario: why could she not see out? Why was this so secretive? What was he hiding? Who was he hiding? Her imagination was going into overdrive and running away with her. All she could do was stare into the abyss that was the interior of the limousine and wonder.

Looking above her head, she found a light and turned it on. She grabbed her handbag and got her notebook out and started writing all these things down. There was a story: her writer's imagination could see it but did she really want this to be a story as this was her life. What she could do was ask Damion these questions once she was in his company at some point this afternoon. The limousine swayed with the contours of the road from side to side, it was quite pleasant. It also allowed her to realize that the road was not straight; she couldn't hear anything from the outside but she did know that wherever they were going was up hill and a winding road. Before she could figure out which knob put the radio on, P. was talking to her again and the limousine was coming to a halt. "We are here."

That was all the explanation that was given. Vicky decided that he didn't really talk to people very often as she had never met anyone who only gave instructions or statements rather than conversation. Yes, she probably was naïve and that was alright with her. She liked her life simple; she had her own complications to work through and didn't need anyone else's.

Once the vehicle had stopped, her door was opened and a bright beam of light came thrusting through the door. It was blinding as the interior was so dark. P. was at the open door extending his hand to help her out, at least he was chivalrous. That put a large smile on her face. Digging into her handbag, she grabbed her sun glasses and put them on, and put her notebook away for later. I was so bright that she imagined this is what it felt like to be hungover and recovering from the night before. Light sensitive for a start and slightly disorientated.

Stepping out of the car, she heard a crunch as her feet touched gravel. In fact, looking around she could see there was a sea of gravel. White gravel that seemed to go on for miles. Taking in the sight of the gravel was nothing compared to the vast landscape and the monstrous, medieval fort that was before her. The towers on either side of the huge front door were so tall that they seemed to be piercing the clouds above. On closer inspection of the front door, there was something odd about it; it was opening but not how you would expect. Rather than opening as a door would, it was coming down to meet the gravel. That was when she noticed that running underneath the front of the fort was water. Or more aptly known a moat. This was a full fledge fort with its own moat! It looked like it had been transported straight out of Europe and transplanted here, wherever here was. Vicky's mouth was open; she couldn't believe what she was seeing, where was she?

Once the drawbridge had landed firmly onto the gravel, she saw him. Damion was walking towards her and she could hear the crunching of the gravel under his feet. She was unable to stop staring at him, even when he was right in front of her. She was still holding onto the opened door of the limousine and couldn't let go. She was in total shock.

"Victoria, I am so glad that you have arrived. Sorry I could not have accompanied you here but I knew you would be in very capable hands with P. Welcome to my home."

That voice was talking to her but she kept looking at him and looking at the fort: could this be real? I mean, who owns a fort? The only people she knew of lived in Europe and were royalty, is that what he was? Was he royal? All she managed to say was, "Hi"

It was kind of pathetic for a response but at least it was one. What did you say to someone who owned a fort? His voice was as amazing as she remembered and she was waiting patiently for him to speak more. She would follow him anywhere if he spoke.

"You must be hungry? I know I am." There was something in that sentence it was not just about food but Vicky couldn't quite place what it was. So instead of answering verbally she nodded her head.

"Please come in and join me. After lunch, I will show you to your room and you can rest if you like." That sounded like heaven: food and rest. Then maybe she could figure out what she was doing here...

Chapter 6

Damion had taken hold of the hand that was clinging to the car door and pried Victoria's fingers from it. His hand was warm to her chilled skin and she felt the heat radiating up her arm and into her body. It was if just that touch alone was a blanket wrapping her in heat. If this is what his hand could do to her just by holding hers then what would it be like to have his body pressing against hers? Her face flushed red and a groan escaped her lips, she really wanted to find out and hoped that it would happen soon. Looking up at his eyes, she could see that he was staring at her again with intensity that was mesmerizing.

Damion didn't say anything else, he just pulled her from the car and started walking hand in hand towards the draw bridge. The crunch from under their feet was the only sound, except from her heartbeat that was crashing against her chest. As they approached the entrance, Vicky became a little frightened by the sheer magnitude of her decision. Looking over her shoulder, she could see the limousine driving away down the white graveled road and, at that point, she realized that this was it. There was no point in dwelling on leaving as that was not an option.

Turning her head back to the imposing fort, Vicky stole a glance at Damion only to find that he was watching her as they walked. Obviously, this was his home so he knew every pebble or gravel, as it were, so he didn't need to worry about falling down. Vicky, however, was not so sure footed and therefore was making a special effort to not embarrass herself by falling face forward into the pristine white gravel. That would not be in her best interest as she was hoping for more than just a meal together. As it was she was not at all sure why she was here or what she had signed up for but she was more than willing to find out.

The sound under foot had changed and, looking down, she realized they were going over the draw bridge: how surreal was that! Again, she wondered who was this Damion person and what did he do to have this! Shaking her head, she just kept walking. Damion had not let go

of her hand and the feeling was wonderful, she really liked how it felt. No one had given her the tingles that were running through her body and the heat. She couldn't explain it.

Once they were over the draw bridge, Vicky looked up to see the ceiling was made of bricks and curved just like a medieval castle. It was like entering a fairytale, or rather a gothic movie set. It didn't take long to walk through and, while doing, so she realized that it was wide enough to have cars pass through it. Once exiting, Vicky had to stop for a minute to take it all in. Before her was the largest checker board she'd ever seen. It was made up of grass and concrete. To her left was a row of wide doors and to her right was a high wall, clearly for balance. She looked back at Damion hoping he might say something about this but he was still watching her without saying anything.

Damion was enjoying watching every expression that Victoria made. It started with when he grasped her hand at the car and the blush that crept up her face, to the wide-eyed, stunned look she had right now looking around the courtyard. He knew that she was waiting for him to explain what was before her but he was enjoying this too much. He never had to explain anything to anyone anymore and would never have that feeling again.

Victoria was different from the others. He had interviewed each and every one of the women that ended up coming to the house and inevitably they had all asked the same questions. "Why a fort, what's that over there, am I the first?" etcetera, etcetera... It had become so tiresome that, after the first few, he had said in the interview that one of his rules was to never ask questions. From the instant they set foot in the house, that had worked a charm. He liked the women to be able to follow directions and if they couldn't then they were gone. He had never had the same woman twice; the list was vast so therefore he never needed too. Also, not one was so exceptional that he took that much of an interest in them; they were a means to an end. If they got something out of it, great but ultimately this was his game not theirs and for the most part no one complained and if they did then they were gone. It was simple: follow the rules and reap the reward. If not then it was over.

Refocusing on Victoria, Damion gently squeezed her hand and pulled her forward to continue walking across the checkered ground towards the main house entrance. Damion was instrumental in every facet of the construction of the house, from the design to the intricate details such as door handles.

Vicky felt the tug on her hand and looked down quickly to make sure that their hands were still joined. She felt Damion pulling her forward and had to tell her legs to move so not to stumble. Walking across the courtyard was an experience in itself as the checkers were hard and soft alternating from concrete and grass. They were walking towards a black door.

Once they reached the door, they stopped. Damion looked at Victoria and smiled while opening the door. This was the start and he was very excited about the next step, or rather what was going to happen later tonight once she had rested and eaten. He found that food and comfort made even the most ridged person a little more pliable. Not that he thought that Victoria was ridged but he knew that she had no idea what she had given to him. He also predicted that she had never done anything like he was going to do to her. In fact, he was sure she that she was a virgin and, if not, she was definitely not experienced.

"Lunch has been prepared for us so we will eat first."

It was not really a question it was more of a statement, much like how P. spoke to her. That brought a crease to her brow but she decided not to think about it too much. She was very nervous and was not sure how she was going to eat in front of him. She was really hungry but didn't want to make a fool of herself. She was a self-proclaimed klutz. Dropping food on herself was a standard affair and spilling her drink was a given. Hopefully lunch was just a small meal, like sandwiches or a salad. She thought she might just be able to handle that and then she could relax for a bit; all this nervous energy was making her jumpy and tired.

Damion led her through the front door and down a long hallway. The walls were carnelian red with what looked like original M.C Escher paintings. The contrast of the black and white paintings and the carnelian red was striking. She was fascinated by this art and always had been. There was something so intricate and alluring about it. It was possible to become lost in the pictures; Vicky specifically loved the Drawing Hands. She didn't see it on the wall but they were moving briskly down the hall. Damion still had her hand in his possession and it felt completely natural.

She was wondering why this was happening and if she had acted rash when they arrived at the largest, brightest room she could see. It was a huge kitchen with an attached conservatory. The walls were white, the cabinet's ash and the counter tops white marble. The whole room seemed to be one reflection after another. The refrigerator, sink, chef's stove and the other appliances were made from stainless steel. Looking to the conservatory, Vicky saw there was a large round table the same color of the cabinets and high back chairs the color of the walls. Through the windows, she could view an expanse of vast greenery and Vicky knew that sitting here with a cup of tea would be magical. She counted six chairs at the table. But, turning back to the kitchen, she didn't see anyone except Damion: where were the staff? She expected there to be staff to serve them their lunch. It definitely appeared that Damion would have staff to take care of this house; it would need to be a team of them.

"Would you care for tea, water, soft drink or something stronger perhaps?"

Bringing Damion back into focus, Vicky responded, "Water is fine."

A short answer would be best from her at this point; she was so nervous and didn't trust herself not to say something ridiculous. Leaning against the island in the center of the room, which was more like a peninsula as the room was so massive; she was able to study Damion without him knowing. He really was gorgeous: he wore faded blue jeans that clearly were loved, a grey polo shirt, not tucked in, and brown flip flops. That surprised her and made her smile: she figured him for a closed-shoe type of guy.

"Why are you smiling? You can share. I want to know what makes you smile," he said walking towards her with a glass of water with a lemon wedge in it.

Unsure how to say what she really was thinking, Vicky decided to play it safe and said,

"I am just very happy to be here" which was a half-truth, she was happy to be with Damion, she was just not sure why she had been flown to this location.

"Hum, not sure that is the real reason for that smile but I shall let it go as I know you will tell me one way or another."

There was an absolute confidence in that statement and, again, a hint of authority behind what was said. She instantly had goose bumps run up her arms and felt the need to look away from his intense gaze.

"Would you like a sandwich or salad: what would you prefer?"

"What kind of sandwich or salad is it?" She didn't really care she was just making small talk: anything would do.

"Well, let's see. There's ham and cheese, turkey and cheese, egg salad and I believe roast beef for the sandwiches and for the salad you can have Caesar or fruit, what appeals to you?"

"How about a turkey and cheese sandwich, please."

Damion was so pleased with how she responded just that little word please meant that it would not be too difficult for him to get her to submit to his whims. With a grin, like the cat that got the cream, he placed her food on the plate provided for him from his chef.

There was no staff here at present as that is what he requested. They would arrive in a couple of hours. That way, it would allow Victoria to become more at ease in his home. In fact, his staff would be needed to assist with some of the preparations for this evening. Just thinking about that stirred desire inside of him and he could feel himself becoming aroused. He didn't want to scare her but he was struggling for control right now and placating her with food was just a filler. After this meal, he would show her to her room and strongly suggest that she get some rest as she definitely would need it. Giving her the plate, he went and got his own food. He was quite happy to serve himself and he was not above taking care of himself. But he did enjoy the finer things in life. Having staff wait on him hand and foot at his home gave him great pleasure. Each one had been selected specifically for their role and they performed it to the letter.

After gathering a sandwich for himself and some water, he motioned for them to sit at the table. It was one of his favorite places to sit and look out onto the gardens. Most mornings, he would grab a cup of coffee and just sit here before starting his day. Like most people, he had a home office which allowed him the luxury of working from home. In it he had all the latest high-tech computers and software available: he could run his empire from it. Sitting here in the morning allowed him to appreciate what he had achieved. It was impossible to see into his property, he had designed it that way, and the views at any time of the year were impressive.

Vicky was still watching him. In fact, she was unable to stop. Damion was just so impressive and the way in which he moved demanded attention. While he fixed her lunch, Vicky noticed how he commanded his task: it was exciting to see. It made her wonder if he commanded every aspect of his life in the same way? Vicky started to think about what it would be like to kiss him; just the thought brought a flush to her face and her nipples to hard peaks. He had to know what she was thinking but she really hoped he didn't. She was still unsure as to why she was there.

Sitting at the table, Vicky took a deep breath and prepared herself to not drop food while eating. Vicky waited for Damion to sit before eating as years of etiquette classes at school had taught her manners and that was one of them.

Damion was impressed as to why she was waiting for him to sit before eating. He knew she was hungry and fully expected her to dive into her food but the unexpected wait was yet again surprising and exciting. Was she a submissive on purpose or was she un-aware of her submissive tendencies? In her eyes, she probably just thought she was being polite, after all, he did make her lunch and she did sit before him. So it was possible that it was just manners but there was just something there... she still had not taken her eyes off him. Normally, that was not allowed. The women were told not to look at him unless he spoke to them directly about eye contact. He was not interested in them as a person and their submission was what he wanted. Total and complete control was expected but with Victoria he loved the way in which she watched him. He could feel her eyes on his skin, caressing and teasing him. He loved that as it had never happened before, mostly due to him not allowing it to. Many women had tried to pursue him for marriage but he was a very wealthy man and too many of them wanted just that, his wealth. He was more than just money; he was a person with feelings and emotions; though he never showed them, not even in business. He prided himself on being level-headed, even under the most severe of pressures.

Victoria was someone he had never believed was possible and the reaction he got just from her looking at him was startling and exciting. However, he did only have her for one week so therefore he was going to make the most of it. Looking at her face, he saw that telltale color that rose from within. Clearly, she was thinking again but what, he did wonder. He knew that Victoria's skin was a canvas and many things could produce the reaction he was seeing in front of him at the table. She was his very own living painting for the week and he couldn't wait to see what and how her skin reacted to what was in her future.

"Please eat; I know you must be hungry. It was an early start and, from what I was told, you slept on your way here. Did you not sleep well last night"? Damion said then proceeded to eat half of his sandwich in one bite.

Vicky was impressed with that. She had never really watched a man eat before, or at least never paid attention to it. It was something everyone did but this was Damion and everything he did was different. She was going to answer his question but had a few of her own.

"No, I didn't sleep well; I had a lot on my mind."

Before allowing Victoria to ask her questions, Damion beat her to it,

"No? Why not, what was on your mind"? He said in between eating and drinking his water.

"Well, how did you know where I lived? And why am I here? Also, where are we?" Vicky hoped that her questions didn't come out as rude but she really did want the answers. Too nervous to eat before getting the answers, she just sat there and continued to watch him.

"Really, you should eat. I will answer your questions but they might not be... no, in fact, I am positive... they will not satisfy you but only produce more questions that, at this moment, I have no intentions of answering. To answer the first one, I know where you live because, when I want something, I make sure I know what and where it is. As to why and where you are; you are in my home and, well you agreed to spend seven days with me. You didn't ask me where, you just took a leap of faith, to which I am very pleased you did. Obviously, you want to be here as at any time you could have said you wanted to go home and you didn't. So please, eat your lunch and enjoy all that I can offer you, this would make me very happy."

He was right. His answers did lead to more questions but he was also correct: she did agree to be with him for seven days and she never asked where. Resigning herself to that, she finally broke the eye contact, which was very difficult to do, and brought the sandwich to her mouth. To say that the sandwich was the best she had ever tasted seemed so cliché but it was true., Maybe it had a lot to do with her hunger but she had a feeling that this was gourmet food and not package food from the local supermarket. Everything complemented one another, from the bread to the meat and cheese. Even the water, which was just water, tasted amazing. Hunger really will play games with you. Smiling again, Vicky took another mouthful of food and moaned with contentment.

"That is a lovely sound, I do hope to hear that a number of times this week," Damion said with that smile that lit up the room.

Embarrassed, Vicky quickly looked out of the window and took in the incredible view. She inhaled, which caused the food in her mouth to go down the wrong tube, which then caused her to start coughing. This had gone from being embarrassing to just total shame. Finally getting it together, Vicky looked back at Damion, praying that that really didn't happen and the coughing fit was just in her imagination. However, the look on his face told her it hadn't.

"Are you alright? Do you need a doctor? I can have one here in ten minutes." Damion was both concerned and amused. He didn't want her to be injured but that certainly was not a reaction he had ever seen, especially just from looking out of a window.

Completely embarrassed, Vicky really just wanted to crawl into a hole and disappear. Here was this gorgeous man who had made her lunch and what did she do? Not only did she choke on the food but she moaned out loud. Now she had to respond to him.

"No. I am fine, no need for a doctor really. This is nothing new for me but most of the time I am by myself so no one sees what I am capable of when eating food." She said in her most assertive way or at least she hoped it was.

I you are sure, then what can I do to make you more at ease? I am sure this is a lot to take in. Would you like to finish your lunch or would you rather just go and rest? I do not mind either way: you just let me know which you would rather do."

"I think I am done with food for now so, if is not too much trouble, I think I would rather go and rest." That sounded good she thought. That way she could hide, even if it was just for the afternoon.

"Okay, if that's what you want. It's not like this is the only meal you will have while you are here. In fact, as you are here for seven days, I am sure there will be plenty of opportunities for you to eat." He said with a knowing smile.

Rising up from the table, Damion motioned for her to do the same and, as he left the plates on the table, Vicky was sure that his staff, who were somewhere, would take care of them. She grabbed her water and followed Damion out of the kitchen.

Chapter 7

Damion and Victoria didn't go down the hall they had come in from but rather left out of what seemed to be another hall way. Following Damion seemed like the most natural thing in the world to do. Yes, this was his house but there was something else, something that she couldn't put her finger on.

This time when she looked up to her right, there was a wall of windows allowing the natural light to invade the hall way. The wall color was the same as the other side but the paintings that hung here where Salvador Dali; again, they looked to be original. The windows looked out onto a large lawn that looked like it was a putting green but she only had a quick chance to look before she was heading up a flight of stairs. Once at the top, Vicky saw another hall way and only one door. Damion stood in front of it waiting for her: she was only a few steps behind him, or so she thought, but apparently not. Once she reached Damion, he opened the door and walked inside. Vicky followed him in.

The first thing she noticed was the size of the room. It was the size of her entire house, with the most beautiful bed standing in the middle of the room. That seemed odd but, other than that, all the furniture was against the walls. It was clear that the bed was the focal point of the room. The floor appeared to be marble tiles in blues and greys and the walls were navy blue. In a small room, this would be overwhelming and would make the room feel cold and small but, with this size, that was not a problem at all. The furniture was very masculine and rather chunky. There was nothing feminine about this

51

room except the billowing duvet and pillows on the bed itself. They were not floral print but rather swirls of blue and grey to match the rest of the room, giving the room a warmth that was unexpected.

"I'm sure that this will be comfortable enough for you to rest. There will be someone to help you with dressing for dinner so please just stay in here. There is an adjacent bathroom for your needs and a selection of books for you to read if you like."

Victoria was not really paying that much attention to what Damion had just said as she was still longingly looking at the bed. Therefore, she was unaware that he had left the room and closed the door. It wasn't until she heard the soft click of the door that Vicky noticed that she was alone. She walked over to the door and turned the knob, hoping to see Damion again, but instead found that the door was in fact locked. Struggling with the door, Vicky was not happy about being locked in and, as soon as she saw Damion again, she would definitely let him know that in no uncertain terms did she ever give permission to be locked inside of a room, opulent and vast as it was; she didn't like the feeling of being trapped. Even though it was hard to feel trapped in a room as large as this.

Sighing in shear frustration, Vicky gave up on the door and stood, hand on hips, looking about the room. Damion had said that there was a bathroom and books but, for the life of her, Vicky could not see a book shelf or another door besides the one she had entered. Walking towards the bed, she kicked off her shoes and dropped her bag and looked about again, hoping that her mind was just playing tricks on her due to her exhaustion. All the adrenalin had left her body once entering this room. It was strange that a room could make you feel something. Yes, she had known that paintings can make you feel emotion but she had not felt that a room could have the same effect. She also expected the floor to be cold but instead it was warm under foot.

"Is this heated?" she questioned out loud, realizing after saying it that no one would answer her. She shrugged and carried on with her exploration of the room.

Walking over to the walls, she ran her fingers along as she walked. As she was not really focusing on the wall, she was surprised to feel a crease in it. Coming back to the crease, Vicky pushed gently and found that it was a door, flush to the wall. There was no door handle for her to hold but once the door pushed all the way in, she was able to see a stark white bathroom fit for a king. Like the bedroom, it was huge, with a claw-footed bathtub in the center of the room, a shower stall against the far wall and a vanity most women would kill for. The lighting was perfect and came on once she entered the room. On closer inspection, Vicky saw a panel on the wall, which allowed for mood lighting and music. High rectangular windows adorned the walls, allowing the natural light in, but they were at the top of the walls, touching the ceiling, so it would be impossible to look out or even be seen from the outside. It allowed for absolute privacy.

Bringing her vision back to the bath, Vicky decided that was exactly what she needed. Being in water had always soothed her and her love of water was one of the reasons she had moved to Florida's coast. To her left was a wall of mirrors, which turned out to be shelves with the books Damion had mentioned. It was also floor to ceiling with towels, all in white, in an array of sizes, from wash clothes to gigantic bath sheets – the ones that she dreamed she had bought for her own house and never got around too. Not able to resist touching them, she felt her fingers being hugged by the sheer thickness of the towel. This was not just a towel; this was an experience.

Laughing at her own pathetic enjoyment of touching a towel, she stripped off right where she stood and turned the water on for a bath. She was surprised that she wasn't cold while waiting for the bath tub to fill; and she was again surprised at how quickly it had filled. Tepidly spearing her foot into the water and feeling the heat, she quickly sunk her entire body into the water. It was much deeper than she originally thought it would be; in fact, her entire body up to her neck was submerged. The heat of the water removed any tension she had had and gave her the comfort she was looking for. Not wanting to wash, or rather not finding any soap to wash, Vicky just sat in the warmth of the water not thinking or anything and just letting the heat do all the work. Resting her head back against the tub, she lifted her hair so it was cascading over the back of the tub, closed her eyes and let out a very contented sigh.

She stayed like that until the water became cool and then reluctantly got out of the tub. Only then did she feel chilly so she grabbed a bath sheet, wrapped in it and made her way over to the bed. Not caring for her nudity, as it was only her in the room, she went over to the bed and took the few steps to climb up onto the bed. Once there, lying on top of the bed, which cradled her, she drifted off to sleep.

Chapter 8

Damion knew that Victoria had not been paying attention to him once they had entered the room. He also knew that him leaving after what he had said would make her want to find him so he had locked the door. This was not to imprison her; it was to keep her away while he and his staff prepared the house for her. Everything he was doing was for her, which was unusual for him. Up to this point, it had always been about him. And yes, ultimately, he was still doing that but he also didn't want to frighten Victoria, whereas the other women's feelings didn't matter. Not that he was a bastard but the others had been well prepared for what lay ahead of them. It had been discussed at length during the interviewing stage. He had stood outside her door for a few minutes until she had given up trying to exit. He heard her exhale loudly.

Damion smiled and walked back down the stairs to his office, where he had called his staff to a meeting. There Sibyl, the house manager and chef, Zara and Philippe, and P. awaited him. Sibyl had been with Damion for many years here at the house and knew how to keep the house just the way in which he liked it. She was a motherly type, who never let anyone be hungry or not cared for. Zara and Philippe had happened by chance, Zara had been one of the first of women to be interviewed to be subservient to Damion but, after the lengthy process, it had come to his attention that yes, she was a sub but she was more interested in participation under his direction. Philippe was Zara's husband and was just as subservient as she was but he knew that Damion could give Zara the one thing he could not. He could not bring himself to dominate her in the same way but was more than happy to watch and participate in Damion's games. Damion never over stood his boundaries within their marriage but while they worked for him, which had been many years, they did as he demanded. P. was... well P. was P. He had left to go and gather the staff and bring them back; nothing went past him that was his job, to be Damion's right-hand man or whatever he needed.

Damion spoke to Sibyl first, "Is everything ready for dinner? Do you need to gather anything else? If so, please let P. know and he shall go and retrieve it for you".

"No, I have everything thanks, am I to serve the food in the dining room or the kitchen?"

"Dining room, and make sure the table is set top and tail. Nothing as a decoration is to be put on it".

"Right as you wish," Sibyl said, with a cheeky smile on her face and she left the room.

"P., make sure that the dining room table is the correct one with the straps and, if not, change it out. Also, I do not want anyone to be seen today or to be seen throughout the week, unless I say."

"No problem, I will take care of it." P. was a man of not many words but if he said he would take care of something then it was done. No need to question it. He too left to take care of the table.

"Zara and Philippe, Victoria is not like the others – she was not part of the list – however, I still want her to be bathed in the same way and when she goes outside to the pool to be cared for in the same manner. Zara, I want you to help her dress every day, as well as styling her hair the way in which I expect. But, more attention is to be had to her: she is to be in a sense of excitement. She is inexperienced in my ways but I want her to be ready at any time. Remember that I shall always be watching, as you know, so you may bring her close but not over. Is that understood?"

With a nod of understanding and eyes brightening, Zara managed to say, "Yes, I understand as you have directed. I shall not disappoint."

"Good, make sure that is the case."

"Philippe, your duties remain the same and as normal. You shall be expected to accomplish those. Again, I can and will repeat: she is not from the list and is not to be treated as if she is. The same applies for you. Handle with care but be firm; I fully expect reluctance from her. Do not allow her to become unattached and to stay in her room alone. Understand?"

"Yes, I understand and kind but firm gloves will be used, be sure of that." Philippe said with absolute assurance.

"Make sure that is the case... And the white is to be worn tonight."

Both Zara and Philippe nodded with understanding and left the room, leaving Damion to himself.

Turning his eyes to the monitors on his desk, he clicked a few buttons and found what he was looking for. There was Victoria sleeping on the bed with a towel wrapped around her. However, once he zoomed in, Damion was able to see that the towel had slipped down across her breasts and was half covering her nipples – the sight instantly brought tightness to his groin. Her deep breaths cemented what he could see; she was sleeping soundly. With that knowledge, he moved to the right of the desk and turned the thermostat down a few degrees. He wanted her to rest but he wanted to see her nipples harden because of him even if he was not directly touching them.

He rewound the video feed and was able to see Victoria's every move and reaction upon entering the room with him. It was evident that, after a time she had found the bathroom and the tub. Damion smiled as he knew there was nothing for her to clean herself with: he had planned it that way. This was to be an experience for Victoria later, which he could not wait to be party to. Fast forwarding a little, he was able to watch her undress rapidly and step tepidly into the tub at first and visibly relax. Yes, that is what he needed from her, to be totally relaxed, as what he had planned for the first night was going to be anything but relaxing for her mentally or physically.

Bringing the feedback to the present, Damion was able to see what he wanted. Victoria's nipples had become erect, which in turn made him moan deep in his throat with want. The room was not so chilled for her to wake but would keep her erect throughout her slumber. Damion found it very hard to not watch her sleep but if he was to give her the attention he wanted this week then he needed to do a couple of hours work. He did keep the monitor on her so he could gaze upon her at his leisure though. He didn't need much pushing to keep looking at her and he was becoming more excited every time he did so as, with her turning from side to side, the towel was slowly moving down her body. It was becoming impossible for him to accomplish any work so he gave up.

He had managed a couple of hours, which meant it was four thirty. That meant that Victoria really needed to start waking up. It was time to begin. Damion turned the thermostat down again to a chilly sixty-five degrees and watched her become awake. He couldn't wait to be besides her when that happened, her becoming awake due to him. He zoomed in again and watched the goose bumps appear on her skin, her eyes began to flutter open and her lips parted. Her tongue ran across the lower lip, playing catch with the upper lip, and she sat up. He was done for. How was he going to not be a mess around her when just that caused him to pant? Deciding that a very cold shower was needed, Damion abruptly got up from his desk and left the office to do just that.

Chapter 9

The first thing that Vicky noticed upon waking up was that she felt cold. The next thing she was aware of was the fact that she was naked and not in her own bed. It took a moment to remember where she was or rather remember that she was in Damion's home somewhere in the world.

Sitting up, Vicky started rubbing her hands up and down her arms trying to create warmth. Glancing down, she could see that her skin had goose bumps and her nipples were so erect. As she was warming her skin, she grazed her nipples and just about leapt off of the bed – the sensation was extreme! She had very sensitive nipples anyway and almost anything could set her off but skin-on-skin touch was almost too much. Moaning out loud, she pulled up the bath sheet to cover herself.

Vicky felt rested and ready for whatever lay ahead of her but she need her clothes. She remembered stripping off in the bathroom so made her way over to where she remembered the door was in the wall. To her surprise, she found the door was closed. She didn't remember doing that but she was very relaxed after her bath so maybe she did? She went in and looked for her clothes. They were not where she thought she had left them. She kept searching to no avail, figured she would use the facilities whilst in there, went to the toilet and tried to remember where she had stripped off.

Coming out of the toilet, she was fully awake now and realized that the entire room was spotless. It looked as if it had never been used or she had not even been in there before. Perhaps one of the staff came in and cleaned up while she was resting and took her clothes as well to be laundered? That was the only explanation she could come up with. Vicky re-wrapped the towel around her and headed back into the bedroom. She started to wander around the room thinking about where clothes might be. She walked over to the wardrobe and opened it. She fully expected to see her belongings but was only to find that the wardrobe was totally vacant. Moving over to the chest of drawers, she began opening them only to find they too were empty. She was becoming a little fractious and nervous: she surely was not going to be left only in a towel for the remainder or the week? There must be clothes somewhere. Heading over to the door, she hoped that it would open but found that it was still firmly closed; now frustration was setting in. Vicky tentatively knocked on the door and said,

"Hello, is anyone out there? I need clothes and would really like to come out please." Even in her own mind, she sounded a little pathetic. Here she was, a grown woman and she was naked and locked in a room. She kind of felt like she was being punished for something but she had no idea what for.

"Hello?" This time she spoke with more force behind it but still no one answered or came to the door.

Feeling totally helpless, she walked over to the bed and sat down. With her new frustration, she was quite warm so she lay flat on her back with the towel open hoping to cool off. It felt as if time was no longer moving and Vicky was trying to calm down so she closed her eyes and took some deep breaths. She decided that obviously she was not going to be locked in here forever but she had

61

no idea what was going on here and once she could talk to Damion, she sure would find out.

As her eyes were closed, she had no idea that someone had opened the door and stood against the wall watching her. She only became aware when she heard a noise, it sounded like a clearing of the throat. Her eyes instantly opened and she grabbed the towel hoping that whomever was in the room had not seen her naked. Sitting up, she looked over to where the noise had come from and found a very tall man standing there. He was dressed all in white, from his white T-shirt to his white shorts, both of which clung to his impeccable body. Vicky was able to see the outline of the taught muscles along his stomach and, her eyes traveling south, she could see the material straining against the definition of masculinity.

An instant gasp escaped from her parted lips and her eyes grew large. Immediately, Vicky brought her eyes to his face and was struck by his incredible intense stare. Those eyes that stared back at her were green and seemed to look right into her. His hair was midnight black and his skin was golden brown, as if kissed by the sun. He had not uttered a word but that one sound and, in that instant, she was aroused.

Philippe had slipped into the room without a sound; that is what was expected of him at all times while there was a woman in the house for Damion's pleasure. Never to be seen or heard unless instructed otherwise, he enjoyed this initial stage as this was the only time he was alone with the intended playmate. Until now, they all had some idea as to what came next; however, with Victoria, this was all new and Philippe was the beginning. He had to make her feel relaxed or rather as relaxed as possible with what was coming next. This first part was incredibly intimate and he wanted this to go as smoothly as possible.

With that in mind, he was watching her and had been since entering the room. She had been lying on her back with the towel open for him to feast on her beautiful body in all its splendor. Even though he was married, he truly had an appreciation for the female form, of which there were many. This job he had with Damion allowed him to make his fantasies come true almost daily and with his wife included.

He was able to allow his eyes to travel up her athletically toned legs to the apex of her thighs where the curls hid the most precious of jewels from sight. Her legs were together, not allowing him to see but his imagination could. Also, within a few minutes, he would see exactly the jewels that were so deftly hidden at the moment. Drawing his eyes up across her flat, toned stomach and up to the perfectly pert and round breasts, he could see that her nipples were a rose pink and ready to be plucked. With his need intensifying, he knew that watching his beautiful wife Zara bringing Victoria to the edge needed to happen sooner rather than later. Victoria's face was at ease but Philippe was on a time schedule so this needed to be swift.

He cleared his throat and watched as the recognition dawned on her face that someone was in the room with her. She immediately sat up and drew the towel around her body as protection. It was too late for that but if she felt better about it he was not going to tell her otherwise. It was probably the most covered she would be for a while. Knowing that his voice would ease her worries, he said, "Bonjour, Victoria. I do hope that you are well rested. However, now we must get you ready for dinner with Mr. Foster. Please stand up and remove the towel from around your body as I have something more appropriate for you to wear."

Vicky was in shock as to how this man had gotten into the room without her hearing anything; it would seem that this was just one more question or mystery of this house. His voice was soothing and she was not sure if it was due to the slight French accent or just his tone. Either way, she was willing to follow his direction, even if she was hesitant to become bare. Thinking about this, she asked,

"Why do I need to remove the towel? Where are my clothes from earlier today and, if you could just provide my suitcase, I have other clothes in there that I can dress in." All the while, she was holding the towel closed with a death grip.

"I am sure that after your rest you would like to shower and freshen up and I am here to take you to the bathing room for that to occur."

"I have a bathroom right here but there seems to be no soap. Could you perhaps just get some for me? That way, I can take a quick shower and be ready in about ten minutes. Oh, and if you could get some shampoo then I could wash my hair as well. I am sure that under the sink there would be a hairdryer I could borrow, thanks."

"Non, you have no need to worry about such matters. All will be provided for you. Now, if you would please remove the towel, we can move to the bathing room and prepare for tonight." Philippe said all this while walking towards Vicky and he brought just a touch of dominance to his voice. He didn't want to overwhelm her but he knew she would not come as willingly as the others had.

Vicky was watching him approach and she was still confused about why they were leaving this room as there really was a perfectly good shower in the bathroom and the whole thing about removing the towel just baffled her. The man, who still didn't give his name, clearly worked for Damion in some capacity but she had no idea what. She was still mulling this over when she felt his warm hands gently but firmly bring her hands out to her sides so to discard the towel.

She reluctantly let go of the towel. All the while, this man was looking into her eyes and he never looked down. At least he was not looking at her nakedness. She didn't realize that over his left arm there was dressing gown for her to change into. He drew the towel away from her reach and replaced it with the most delicate dressing gown. Bringing her arms through the sleeves felt like little feathers tickling her skin and made her shiver. Once upon her shoulders, he drew the front closed and secured it with the belt. If she had the gumption to look down she would have seen that this garment was completely sheer and all of her was in view.

Philippe enjoyed the view this garment allowed. The others all had worn a more conventional dressing gown but this one had been picked out specifically for Victoria. It bared no weight and was only long enough to meet her mid thighs. The color was pure white but was only able to see the color when not being worn. Damion had wanted her to be on show at all times and this certainly did that. Her body was walking art to be admired for all that were able to gaze upon it. Gently pulling her hand while he walked to the door, Phillippe didn't look back. He felt her reluctance but continued on.

Vicky seemed to have lost her tongue and was not able to ask where they were going. She was being led by this man to what he had called the bathing room, whatever that was, and she was just going along with it. She definitely had many questions for Damion when she did eventually see him but for now, with this man, she felt very comfortable… if only she had asked his name. Gently shaking her head, she decided that at least she would find this out:

"What is your name, if you please, I really like knowing who is taking me to the bathing room, whatever that is. And, as this is all new to me, I am feeling rather lost, so just normal conversation helps me when I am nervous." She said to his back.

Turning his head over his shoulder, the man replied, "My name is Philippe all will be well you shall see." He smiled as he reached for a door and began to open it.

Vicky was at least pleased that he had given his name to her, a small victory in this strange day. She still wasn't pleased about being locked in a room and not able to have her belongings but with Philippe she was reassured in some small way.

Following him out of the bedroom and down the hall, Vicky was impressed with the furnishings. She had thought that Damion was a traditionalist but his taste in décor was quite eclectic, ranging from ultra-modern with sleek lines to chunky, raw, organic furnishings.

Philippe led them down a different set of stairs and at the bottom there was a round table in the middle of the floor. On top of the table sat a glass dome with a bell encased inside. Victoria was not sure what to make of it and figured it was some decorative art and really didn't give it much more thought. She was more interested in where she was going and what a bathing room was... This was alien to her. This whole thing was alien to her and she had to keep reminding herself to be open minded and remember that she had willingly decided to do this for a week.

Philippe was happy to be leading Victoria to the bathing room as his part in the beginning ritual was just starting. Inside was Zara and she had her part to play in the preparations; he loved watching his wife work. If you could call it that. It was much more pleasure than actual work and, undoubtedly, they would revel in it once they were done.

Chapter 10

Philippe took Victoria down the stairs and around the corner to the other hallway. This house was a maze of hallways; he opened to door on the right and brought Victoria in with him. Once she was in, he closed the door firmly and made sure it locked shut. This activated the recording camera so Damion was able to watch; as Philippe knew he would. Damian always watched but with Victoria he was different; more intense about everything to do with her. Even down to what she was to wear. Normally he left it up to Zara to decide but with Victoria he had made specific arrangements for her wardrobe while she was here.

Vicky stopped abruptly when she heard the door lock. What was it with this house and locked doors she wondered? She looked around the room and was taken by the sheer size. Again, these rooms where enormous. The walls where tiled white and the floor was tiled white, and in the center of the room was a chair like you would see at the hairdressers. Instead of there being padding for comfort, it was just the stainless-steel frame with a stainless-steel seat attached. It did not look comfortable at all and Vicky had no clue as to what it was for. She didn't see a bath or a shower stall anywhere, not even along the walls. What she did see was that to get to the chair you had to go down two steps and there next to the chair was possibly the most beautiful woman Vicky had ever seen. She, like Philippe was wearing white clothing. She had on a white, spaghetti-strapped tank top and the briefest white boy shorts Vicky had ever seen. Her hair was a rich mahogany color with caramel high lights; Vicky found that she wanted to run her fingers through the soft strands that hung long down the woman's back. Her feet were bare, as were Vicky's and Philippe's. Only then did Vicky notice that where the woman stood looked to be the biggest bath tub imaginable. To fill that must be hell on the hot water tank! Still, she couldn't figure out what the chair was for.

"Welcome Victoria, please come down so we can start," said the woman in the middle of the room. Her accent was American and raspier than Vicky expected. However, nothing could have prepared her for any of what was going on in this house.

Vicky was drawn to this woman, not that she had ever felt anything for another woman other than friendship. But, the idea that she might touch or be touched by this woman sent warmth through her body. What would it be like to touch her skin? Was it as soft as it looked? Under the lights it was so shiny. How was that possible? Again, Vicky heard the voice speaking to her from the woman in the middle of the room; Vicky was momentarily rooted to the spot.

With a gentle hand at the small of her back and a glance over her shoulder, Vicky proceeded down the two steps with Philippe following her with his hand still on her back. Was it to make sure that she would go further into this peculiar room? Or so that she would not try and leave the room? Either way, Vicky liked the contact of someone touching her, she realized that human contact was something she had gone without for so long. Even though she craved Damion's touch with every fiber in her being, it had been too long since anyone had made contact with her skin. All of her own doing, she really never made any effort to invite such a thing and really never gave it any thought but having Philippe's hand on her had a calming effect. Something she didn't think would be possible considering the situation.

Once down the steps, Vicky immediately felt a coolness to her back and realized that Philippe had moved away, not wanting to avidly look for him she looked at the floor feeling very shy and unsure what to do.

"Look up, Victoria. Look at me and only at me. I am Zara. I will be taking care of you in almost all ways. Know that everything I do is for your comfort and your pleasure. Like most people in this house, I have a task to perform and my task is you. I take great pride in my task and I promise that you will be cared for with the most thorough care I can provide. Now let's get started."

Zara: that was her name, well at least Vicky knew what her name was. What did she mean take care of her? Finding her strength, Vicky asked,

"What do you mean take care of me? What task? I have only seen Damion, Philippe and now you. Are there many others that work here? What's going on I don't understand? I was led to a room and locked in. I took a bath then laid down and when I woke up my clothes were missing and none of my personal things where anywhere to be seen. The next thing I know, there's a man in my room! How he got in, I don't know. He dresses me in this dressing gown and brings me here. But I don't really understand what is going on, are you able to tell me?" Vicky held her breath, hoping this beautiful woman would give her answers; anything, at this point, would be something she could hold onto.

"I can tell you that your belongings are safe and nothing has happened to them. You won't see anyone in the house unless instructed too. It is the way; as I said, we all have a task to perform and very few are visible at all times. What we are doing is preparing you for Mr. Foster. You shouldn't be afraid as no harm will come to you. It is my understanding that you came here willingly so please, do not fret. Let us care for you. I promise that you will enjoy it. It may be something you have never experienced before but allow yourself this time to be open to new things. Is that not what this is all about for you anyway? Giving yourself to new experiences?"

Everything that Zara said was true. Vicky did agree this. Well, she agreed to come away with Damion for seven days, what "this" was remained to be seen... but Vicky was pretty sure that Zara had no intention of hurting her nor would she allow Philippe to harm her either. With that being said, she let out a shaky breath and nodded. Not all of her questions had been answered but really the only person that could reply to them all was Damion, and from what Zara had said, she would be seeing him at some point today.

"Okay, what do you need me to do?" Vicky asked nervously.

"All I need you to do is relax and let me do what needs to be done. Do not fear the unknown, you might feel unsure but know that pleasure is always the goal." Zara said, while walking the short distance towards Vicky.

Once in front of Vicky, she was able to see that Zara was the same height as her but where Vicky had fair skin, Zara, like Philippe, was sun kissed. Vicky could see that Zara filled out her white tank top and her breasts where larger than Vicky's. Not that she wasn't happy with her own breasts; they were fine, but Vicky wanted to see Zara's. This made Vicky blush: she had never been that into women. She was able to see the beauty in the woman's form but she had never been attracted to a woman before. Perhaps it was just the moment she was in right now. It was all about experiencing new things: that is what she had agreed to. Anyway, who was to say that that was even a possibility. As it was, she was standing in front of this woman waiting for something to happen but what she had no idea.

Just then there was a noise coming from behind her; it was the sound of running water. Her feet had warmth encasing them. Looking down, she saw water around her feet and was inching up her legs. The huge bath tub they were standing in was filling up quickly. Much faster than she thought was possible. The plumbing here must be incredible, well of course it was. It was clear that Damion had more money than anyone she had ever met so if he wanted a quick-filling, enormous bath tub then that is exactly what he got. Vicky started to giggle: what a thing to think of right at this moment.

"Tell me why you are giggling? It is a lovely sound but I am curious to what the reason is?" Philippe said from somewhere behind her. Just as Zara had requested, Vicky did not take her eyes off her to look for Philippe but simply answered,

"It's silly really, I am just impressed with the speed of the water rising. But I suppose it is not impossible if you have the right plumbing." All the while she was trying to look at Zara but she kept looking down.

Zara raised her hand to Victoria's face and lifted it so she could look into Vicky's eyes. Yes, she was not like the others. Victoria was not as self-assured as the others and she had the most expressive face Zara had ever come across. This was going to be an amazing journey with this lovely creature.

Vicky had blushed when looking at Zara's chest: it had made her nipples harden to points waiting to be caressed. Unlike the others, when Victoria did touch eventually did touch her, Zara knew there would be fire under those fingertips. Stealing a glance at Philippe, she could see that Victoria had an effect on him as well. There was no jealousy there between them only pleasure.

Keeping her eyes on Victoria, Zara held her eye contact in place and brought her hands to the sash at the front of Vicky transparent dressing gown. It was clear that Victoria had not once looked down at what she was wearing as she certainly would not have been too comfortable with the nudity. Damion liked this one. Unlike the others, having her viewed at all times was a new thing. Not that Zara was complaining: Victoria was beautiful. Her figure was athletic and most pleasing to the eye. Pulling at the sash and removing it allowed for the gown to open and bare her cleavage. Looking down, Zara's eyes followed the path to the apex of Vicky's legs, Zara saw that Victoria did not shave all of her hair, this would change. Damion wanted to see all of her when he wanted to and to do this she must be prepared. Zara felt her own sex tighten with anticipation, there was heat there just mentally preparing Victoria for Damion. The water was rising and was at their knees, Zara walked Victoria back towards the chair. She had seen the confusion in Victoria's eyes to what this was for. No one ever knew what it was but it soon became clear... not everyone liked it and some just downright refused and those ones were immediately taken home.

Victoria decided to trust Zara: she was doing her best to not take her eyes off her like Zara requested. They were walking backwards and the warm water was now at their knees. They stopped when Victoria's bottom touched something cold. Not able to stop herself, Vicky looked around and saw that she was slightly perched on the strange metal seat. Quickly looking back at Zara with question in her eyes, Vicky was confused; was she to sit down? If so why?

"Am I to sit here?" Vicky asked.

"Yes, you are. Do not be afraid, just sit back and relax: this is all about you and your pleasure." Zara said with a smile, she was very much looking forward to what was about to happen. With that, Zara slid the dressing gown down Victoria's arms and pulled it away from her body. Without taking her eyes off of Victoria, Zara threw the clothing to the ledge away from the rising water.

Philippe now stood behind the chair totally focused on his beautiful wife, Zara. The amount of love he had for this one woman was incredible; he never thought it was possible to feel this way about anyone. He enjoyed preparing the women for Damion but it was watching Zara that did him in: he would do anything for her. He was a man after all and being able to touch and caress other women besides his wife was never a job; it was pure pleasure for him as well. Once they handed them off to Damion, what he and Zara would do would be magical. This was the best form of foreplay he could ever imagine.

Without realizing it, Vicky's dressing gown had been removed and she was sitting on the chair. It was cold on her bottom but only for a second as warm water now caressed her cheeks. It truly was impressive the speed in which this tub was filling. She was lying back trying to keep her eyes open but no longer could do it. She sighed out loud as the water surrounded her. When she opened her eyes, she saw that Philippe was at her head with his hands in her hair and there was an amazing aroma in the air which Vicky soon realized was shampoo. It was the most intoxicating smell she had ever smelled and instantly she relaxed. Philippe's fingers where doing things to her head that she didn't think was possible, never had having her hair washed been such an incredible experience.

While Philippe was taking care of her hair, Zara was applying soap to a sponge, mixing the aromas was a heady thing. Bringing Victoria's legs up, Zara settled them in the specially designed heel slots: the chair was very much like a gynecologist's examination table with stirrups for the feet. The difference was this chair was specially designed for what was about to take place: washing Victoria. Zara would start at the soles of her feet and work her way up. The idea of covering Victoria's body in a soapy film and then rinsing that off brought Zara closer to the edge of sexual excitement. She was anxious to get started and stole a quick glance at Philippe, who too was sexually aroused. Drawing her eyes down to his white shorts, Zara could see just how aroused he actually was. There was a damp mark and it was not from the water... Smiling at her adoring husband, Zara flicked him a naughty smile that promised their own playtime and started to draw the sponge up Victoria's foot. She noticed that Vicky's nails were already painted with the French tip style; Zara was pleased that she would not have to paint them and figured that if Vicky's toe nails were painted it was a good chance that her finger nails where as well.

Damion wanted his playmates just so and it was Zara's job to make that happen, from the softness of their skin to the shine of their hair and everything in between. He was very

specific about his tastes and with Victoria he was even more so. Most of the time, Damion had Zara pick out the clothing but with Victoria he had already ordered an array of clothing. Dressing her was going to be interesting: Zara just hoped that Victoria could be open minded about this experience, starting with what she was about to do to her.

Zara was gently running the sponge up Victoria's leg and had her other hand following behind the sponge. Victoria's skin was soft and only had slight stubble of hair growth; this was going to be an easy fix. Zara deftly reached behind her back to her pouch and grasped the razor. Looking at Victoria's face, Zara was able to see that she was completely at ease for the moment. Therefore, she ran the razor up her leg making a clearing of soap on her way up the leg. Glancing again at Victoria, Zara was making sure that the look of relaxation did not leave her face before continuing with her northern-traveling sponge and razor. Having completed the one leg, she moved to the other in the exact same fashion. Only when Zara was at the junction of her thighs did Victoria seem to come out of her trance. At that moment, Zara and Philippe's eyes met and Philippe took hold of Victoria's shoulders to restrain her from sitting up. This was the most crucial moment as it was imperative to make Victoria as comfortable with this invasion as possible. Zara looked to Philippe for him to become the dominant in this moment and, as usual, he didn't fail.

Philippe knew the exact moment when Victoria came out of her trance of relaxation: her body visibly became rigid and her head started to lift up. He placed his hands on her shoulders in a non-threatening manner, which allowed him to gently but firmly speak in her ear and say,

"You must not move. Listen to my voice only and concentrate on what my hands are doing to your shoulders. Feel how they work your tight muscles and how they give under my touch. Close your eyes and allow yourself to feel every part of my fingertips working those muscles."

Victoria was lost in the heady experience of her hair and body being washed so thoroughly that it took her a minute to realize that Zara was at the apex of her thighs, what could she possibly doing there? Her eyes had flown open and she had started to sit up. Very quickly, she was able to see that Zara had something in her hand other than a sponge and, at that moment, she realized it was a razor. Did Zara mean to shave her down there? Victoria had already, in preparation, shaved her bikini line or so she thought. All of a sudden, Philippe's voice was in her ears and what he was asking her to do was so hypnotic that she lost the ability to question out loud what was going on, as well as just feeling totally relaxed as if this was an everyday experience for her.

There was that word again, experience. It would seem that everything about this place was just that. Just as Philippe had said, Vicky began to focus on feeling his magic fingers doing the work on her muscle told herself to give into whatever Zara was about to do. For some reason, she was not shocked but rather excited about the proximity that Zara was to her most intimate area. So much so that she could feel warmth and her body's reaction began to unfold. The walls of her channel began to tighten and moisture began to gather. Sighing out loud, Victoria was looking forward to what awaited her next. She gave herself to Philippe then and just waited.

Zara had been watching Philippe intensely as he managed to talk Victoria down from her immediate fear. As usual, the sound of his voice and the touch of his strong fingers did the trick. Only once he had given her a brief nod letting her know that he was in control of Victoria did Zara begin. Looking down at Victoria's downy hair in the perfect V, Zara's lips parted. She had never actively wanted to taste any of the playmates. Yet, she had done so under Damion's instruction. However, Victoria was the first to invoke that kind of response. It was obvious to Zara that she had shaved her bikini line but Damion wanted to see everything, and so did Zara. She gently placed her one hand with the sponge on the hair and made sure there was enough there to make shaving a smooth action. Once doing so, Zara began to shave all the hair off except for a slender strip about an inch-and-a-half in length and half-an-inch in width. It looked like an exclamation point without the dot.

Placing the sponge in the pouch at her back, she brought her free hand to feel the skin that had been hidden by the hair. Zara gently ran her fingers over the fresh skin and felt her own sex tighten. If this is what the top felt like then what would the actual center of pleasure source feel like? Quickly gathering the sponge again, Zara soaped the inner sanctum of Victoria's most treasured point on her body. This was an area that clearly had never been bare nor seen by many, Zara imagined. For the first time, Zara felt thrilled to be the first at being so close to it. One at a time she pulled the outer lips taught, allowing her to run the razor over them removing all hair. Not only from there but from the other pleasure point – that Zara was convinced had never been seen, let alone readied for the attention it was sure to receive – leaving Victoria completely bare.

Without thinking and just going on instinct, Zara softly blew air along Victoria's bare skin. Then she was able to see the inner muscle contract and a sheen appeared: a sure sign that Victoria was aroused. Like with the top, Zara used her free hand to caress the bare skin and she could feel the heat and slickness of Victoria's juices. Zara couldn't help herself and brought her mouth to the inviting slit.

She looked up at Philippe, who was watching her and who had moved his hands to Victoria's breasts and was giving them the attention that she clearly was enjoying. Victoria's nipples were two peaks standing tall and erect; Philippe was purposely avoiding them, as that added much more to the tease. Zara was unable to stop herself. She ran her tongue up Victoria's slit and heard a moan of pure pleasure escape her mouth. After all this was part of her job, to keep Victoria at that heighted, sexually aroused point at all times. The fact that Zara was enjoying it was added pleasure for her.

Knowing that more was to come, Zara pulled herself away reluctantly. She knew she would have her turn with Victoria. In the meantime, Zara slipped her fingers into her tight white shorts and felt her need and wetness. She gathered some on her fingers, reached over and placed them into Philippe's open waiting mouth. They were going to have an intense private session very soon... in fact, as soon as Victoria was handed over to Damion at dinner. The first night Damion always played alone. The fact that he wanted Victoria dressed was different but he did want the special table ready for dinner. That was not usually used so early on.

Removing her fingers from Philippe's mouth, Zara started to speak to Victoria. "Come up slowly as we must dry you off so you do not get a chill. Then, you and I will go back to your room and get you ready for dinner with Damion."

Vicky opened her eyes as soon as she heard Zara speak, had she just dreamed all that had just happened or was it real? Looking down her body, she could see a blush all across her skin and her bikini line was no more. In fact, there was really no hair to be seen except the smallest line of hair that really didn't make any sense at all. Why not just shave everything off? Bringing her eyes up to Zara, Victoria was feeling suddenly shy. Again, looking down at her body she was completely naked and feeling very vulnerable. It was a strange feeling as she really did enjoy what had just transpired but there was still that niggling question of doubt: was she suppose too? Should she feel excited that two complete strangers had been attending to her so intimately?

Beginning to panic, Victoria was about to say something when Zara's warm hands reached down and took hold of her own. Looking up again into Zara's eyes she felt herself relax just a little as a towel appeared around her shoulders. Philippe was drying her off while Zara just held her hands. It was oddly comforting, the human contact provided Victoria the calm even during what she felt was an unusual circumstance.

Zara gently pulled Victoria into a standing position. She knew the moment that Victoria began to panic again and instinct took hold: Zara somehow knew that skin-on-skin contact would appease Victoria. While Philippe towel-dried Victoria's body, Zara kept a soft but firm grasp of her hands and kept eye contact with her. Victoria clearly was very susceptible to contact and was incredibly sensitive, which was both intriguing and exciting. Obviously, Zara knew that Damion had been watching what had happened in this room; he would not be cross with her as she was only performed her task that he himself had set. Even though she had taken a slight liberty how could he refuse Zara that one exquisite taste? Zara could feel herself becoming aroused even more and broke eye contact just for a moment to glide her eyes down Victoria's beautiful body. Yes, Zara could not wait to have her all to herself even just for the next hour while she continued with the preparations for Damion.

Philippe had finished drying Victoria and had re-dressed her in the same dressing gown she had arrived in. He could see the heady look in his wife's eyes and knew that she was going to enjoy what was next. This in turn would make their interaction later on more feral and explosive. He himself could feel the pulse of the thick heavy vein that was taught along his hard shaft. It strained against the tight white shorts that now were transparent due to the bathing that just transpired. They would both disappear for a time while Victoria was readied for Damion and he would take himself to their quarters and ready himself for what he was going to do to his beautiful wife.

With one last look at Philippe and a non-verbal "see you soon", Zara smiled at Victoria and looked her over in the dressing gown with approval; she really was beautiful in it. Even though it was transparent and gave no amount of modesty, somehow it was even more alluring. The way every curve could be seen and the junction at the apex of her legs was a gift for the eyes. The slender vertical hair line was a tease of what lay beneath.

Leading Victoria out of the room and up to where she had been before felt like it took a life time. Zara glanced back at Victoria to reassure her as she continued to the room. Before climbing the stairs, she felt Victoria hesitate and looked back to see why. She was staring at the round wooden table with the bell under the glass encasement. Hopefully Victoria wouldn't ask about it, this was not something she ever wanted to talk about. By gently tugging on Victoria's hand, Zara had her moving again in silence and, once up the stairs and in the room, Zara led her to a chaise lounge that was near the end of the bed and said,

"Have a seat; I shall be but a moment. I must gather a few things before I begin. Do not be alarmed, like I said before, this is all about pleasure and you embracing new experiences."

Before Victoria could speak, Zara had left the room through a different door, so she sat down and wondered about the table she had seen down stairs. It was a beautiful wooden table and what was on it in the middle was perplexing. It looked like an antique, handheld bronze bell encased within a glass dome; why would that be?

Nothing else was on the table but that. Perhaps it was extremely valuable, like everything else in this house. Looking around the room, Victoria could see that the furnishings were clearly expensive so that must be the same for the bell. Perhaps it had historical meaning or had been passed down in Damion's family for generations. Whatever the reason Victoria was intrigued and she would ask Zara, hopefully she would get some answers, as so far nothing really had been explained to her other than this was an experience she was to be open to and explore for her pleasure.

What that meant was still somewhat of a mystery. Yes, she had enjoyed being bathed... no, it was more than enjoyment; it was intense and frightening all at the same time. Not something that she would have ever expected to happen to her but she found herself wanting more; of what, she was unsure, but her body was still reeling from the bathing room. Zara had said she was going to gather some things, what did that mean?

Sitting on the cream-colored chaise lounge, Victoria looked around the room again. It was the same room she was initially led to and subsequently locked in but, for some reason, she was not feeling annoyed. She was not sure how to describe the feeling and no sooner had she started to analyze her feelings when Zara reappeared carrying a basket with items in it. Unable to help herself, Victoria stood and started towards Zara only to be stopped with Zara's command.

"I asked you to sit and I meant it. Please follow my instructions. It is important that you are able to follow what I say. I will do you no harm but you are entrusted into my care for a length of time and within that time I have tasks to perform. You will be having dinner with Mr. Foster shortly and I am here to help you get ready. While you are staying here I shall be dressing you. Think of me like a chamber maid of old. You are to not dress yourself or bathe yourself; I will do that for you and, at times, Philippe shall help. However, mostly I shall be taking care of you. Also, you will be dressed in the clothes provided for you each day. Your personal things are safely stowed and, when the seven days are up, they shall be returned to you; this I promise you."

All the while Zara was talking to Victoria, she was walking towards her and when Zara told her to sit that is exactly what Victoria did. For some reason, she didn't want disappoint Zara. She had hoped that perhaps she could explore the sensation of being with Zara in a more private scenario. Shaking her head, Victoria was so confused: what was she thinking? She was totally into Damion and could not wait to see him. So why was she thinking about being with Zara in anyway?

Zara could see that Victoria was battling with herself; this however, was not a war she could win. Everything that was done here was planned and executed by Damion and the selected few, of which Zara was one.

Seeing that she needed to get control of Victoria before she had a panic attack, Zara placed the basket a few feet away from Victoria and reached for her hands. Immediately, Zara sensed the change in her and when she looked into her eyes the confirmation was there. Zara could also see that Victoria had questions but Zara did not want to talk, she wanted to start and keep Victoria on the precipice of falling, which was about to start. Letting go of her for a moment, Zara reached back for the basket which contained a body lotion scented with Vanilla Verbena, a hair towel, a hair brush and a hair dryer. The lotion was picked specifically for Victoria, unlike the others as they had all been given the same body lotion scented with roses. Gently pulling Victoria to the edge of the chaise, so that her bottom was resting on the edge, Zara parted Victoria's legs allowing Zara to slip to a kneeling position between Victoria's opened legs. Dragging the basket closer to her, Zara returned to stare directly at Victoria, and letting go of her hand, she said,

"You must trust me and your own reactions. Yes, this is all new to you, but to explore outside of our mundane lives is what living is about"

While saying this, Zara had undone the belt on the dressing gown and, with Victoria's legs parted, the gown now gaped open making visible a clear vertical path of skin in the middle of her body.

Tracing her fingers from just above the now-cut pubic hair and up to Victoria's chest, Zara slowly started to remove the gown by bringing it down her arms so that it sat around Victoria's bottom. Once that had been achieved, Zara looked away briefly to grab the lotion bottle. She started at Victoria's feet, making sure that no part of Victoria's body was left out. Once the feet and lower legs had lotion applied to them, Zara stood and had Victoria do the same. Zara took a step back, bringing Victoria with her so she was not resting by the chaise but instead free to move all around her. Kneeling once more, Zara was now eye level with Victoria's most private area of her body, she could feel her own self becoming aroused. Zara spread her legs slightly to release some of the building pressure then continued with applying lotion to

Victoria's legs, which were smooth and taught. Working the lotion into her skin was a joy.

Vicky was in a state of sheer pleasure: having someone rub lotion onto her body was a great feeling, and the smell was just beautiful. Clearly, like everything else, this too was not cheap. Savoring the moment, she momentarily forgot that a woman was doing this to her until she felt feather-like touching at the skin that had just been shaved. It was so incredibly sensitive: it was almost too much to take. It took every part of her strength to not fall over but, like Zara had said, she really was giving into the new sensations and feelings and found herself immersed in it. A moan escaped her lips without her own knowledge as those incredible fingers worked their magic all over her body until there was not a place not covered with the magical sent of whatever the lotion was.

Victoria was brought out of her private world with a gentle tug which had her moving towards a vanity. Once seated in front of the vanity, her hair received the same attention as the rest of her body. This time though, it was towel dried and brushed through. Zara was drying Victoria's hair and styling it: this was something that she never did; in fact, she really didn't dry her hair as it was too much of a hassle and not something she liked doing. However, having it done for her… that, she liked very much! Perhaps she could get used to this. And, mentally giving over to everything Zara suggested was becoming easier than she thought it might. Looking at Zara through the mirror, she asked,

"Do you enjoy what you do? Have you done this before? Have you always been with Damion?"

"So many questions you ask. Yes, I do enjoy my work but to be honest this is one of the times that I feel more than I would normally. No, I have not always been with Mr. Foster but I am very happy to be here doing this with you. I am not with Mr. Foster in the way you might think but have been here for a number of years."

While answering Victoria, Zara was still preparing her hair so it would be easily dried. She also rather enjoyed watching Victoria in the mirror; she seemed completely oblivious that she was sitting naked in front of the mirror. She truly was a breath of fresh air. Her entire being was so naïve in a fragile way. Zara just hoped that this experience would not break her. This would be easy to do with someone like Victoria as she was so inexperienced and didn't have a clue to what was before her. Zara knew that Damion would not intentionally hurt her or cause her pain but he would need to be extra careful with this one. She was like a delicate orchid and could wither without care.

Watching Victoria's body move as Zara brushed her hair was a dance in its self. Again, Zara was becoming aroused and her gaze was drawn down Victoria's body to her breasts. The gentle bob of them and her rose bud nipples standing tall were due, not to just the temperature in the room – which was meant to have slight chill to it – but also as Victoria was riding the wave of arousal herself. Unlike Zara, Victoria was not sure how to handle this but Zara had a feeling many pep talks were being had within Victoria's head. Zara couldn't help but watch for a reaction and she was rewarded with the tell sign of Victoria's skin becoming flush with color.

Knowing that she too was being watched, Zara made sure to perform her task efficiently and had Victoria's hair dried and styled in remarkable time. Grasping Victoria's hand and walking her back to the bed, Zara walked over to the cupboard and pulled out the red dress that had been specifically made for Victoria. The gown was a glorious, full length satin and sheer combination that would skim over her delicate skin. Incredibly light that would barely be felt on her body, it would hide away her most intimate of parts but would display her wonderful breasts to their best advantage. The blood red gown was most definitely one of a kind. Zara walked back over to Victoria and was helping her get into it when she was asked another question,

"Should I not be wearing under garment? I mean I've heard of people going commando but I have never done it. I'm not too comfortable going to dinner with nothing underneath this dress."

Zara could see the discomfort in her eyes; however, she was not to wear anything under the gown, that was always the case.

"You will be fine, I promise you. I take care of you and your clothing and, at this time, nothing but the dress and the shoes that will be on your feet are all you need to have dinner. Relax; remember this is all an adventure so go with it, do not think of this as any other dinner you have attended. Mr. Foster has the most splendid dinners and the chef most definitely prepares magnificent food to tempt the palate. Let's finish getting you ready so you can go and enjoy the splendors to be had downstairs."

Vicky was still not sure about the whole no-underwear thing but so far everything that Zara had said was true and this was about new adventures. So, having Zara help her into the most beautiful dress she had ever seen was just one more thing to do.

The dress was exquisite. It molded to every curve of her body in a way that she didn't think possible. The color was the color of blood and made her pale skin stand out in a stark contrast. It had the most plunging neck line she had ever seen on a dress, one that went all the way to the waist of the dress giving her an incredibly deep V with her breasts being constantly hugged by the thin fabric that barely covered them. The only way she was not naked was the sheer material that had the most delicate floral detail over the nipple area. The skirt of the dress was made of light, satin fabric that allowed movement when walking. In fact, the bottom of the dress seemed to dance along with her while she moved. There were slits up the skirt to about mid-thigh. It was rather daring and the most overtly sexy piece of clothing that she had ever worn. When Vicky looked at the back of the dress in the mirror her entire back was bare and the line of the dress cumulated in another V this time at the top of her bottom. You didn't actually see her bottom but it plunged so low it was impossible to not imagine that it was visible.

With a twirl Vicky saw that the way the panels of the skirt flowed out and looked like petals on a flower. This was the most delicate and beautiful dress she had ever worn. She felt like a vixen even if it was only a fleeting moment. Looking again at herself in the mirror, she was suddenly very nervous and didn't want to go anywhere. Zara was placing her shoes on her feet and, looking down, Victoria saw they were the highest heel she had ever worn. They were black as night and sparkled. The combination looked like stars on a cloudless night. Lifting her foot and seeing the underside, she knew that they were extremely expensive as they had the red- lacquered sole. Anyone who knew anything about shoes knew what the red sole meant. They were designed by one of the most sought-after designers around, Christian Louboutin. His trade

mark sole was known across the globe and right know they were on her feet! She wore no jewels or make up but in this outfit clearly the dress was the feature.

"You are ready; we will go down to the dining room. Come, all will be well. Do not look so frightened; this is just the beginning." Zara said with a glint in her eye and a smile in her voice.

Victoria really did feel beautiful but what if it was not enough for Damion? She was so ready for him with want and she hoped he felt the same about her. Yes, she was so frightened it almost felt like lambs to the slaughter: she was a no-one and he was so dynamic and seemed always in control over everything. She had to remind herself that it was only dinner so there was nothing to worry about. All the preparations seemed a tad extreme, much as she thoroughly enjoyed it all to her sheer amazement. But this is what the super-rich did, right? They dressed up formally for dinner so this was the normal, or so she hoped. With one last look in the mirror, she steeled herself and followed Zara out of the room.

Chapter 11

Zara knew that Victoria was having second thoughts; it was written all over her face. If she could handle this then what was to come might be easier for her to accept. Knowing how aroused Victoria was would be a great help, as everything was intended to enhance her every sense.

Zara was heading down the stairs and every so often she would check to make sure that Victoria was indeed following her. Once they reached the bottom, she headed for the dining room. To her amazement, the table that was there was not the one usually in place, at least, not until the next night. Hopefully hiding her reaction, she led Victoria into to the room where Damion was waiting. He was watching for them to enter, again not something that he normally did.

Once they were in the room, Zara stood off to the side to allow Victoria to enter. Zara watched Damion's reaction with interest. It was obvious that this lady was very different from the others that had been and gone before her. His reaction was palpable in every sense of the word. His eyes dilated and his cool demeanor lapsed for just as brief moment. It was barely imperceptible –in the time to blink an eye – but it was not enough to actually notice unless you were really looking for it.

In the room there was ambient lighting, soft glows of yellow light permeated the space which focused on the spectacular table in the center of the room. There was what seemed to be light classical music playing, just audible to hear but not enough to drown out any conversation of the room. Damion was standing at the head of the table with his hands truly gripping the high backing of his chair. His knuckles were slightly blanched white with the force of his grip, again just for a moment in time. To anyone else he looked to be perfectly in control; however, Zara knowing him, knew this to be false. He was every bit as shaken as Victoria was.

The difference was that he could pull it together faster than she could. He also had orchestrated this entire event and dictated every nuance.

The dining table was a special table that usually came out later on in the session of play and it did surprise Zara that it was out now. She was unsure if Victoria would be ready for that particular prop this early on but it was not for her to voice or even have an open opinion as it was it was out of her job description.

Looking up at Damion, Zara saw the nod of dismissal and was happy to leave and find Phillippe. She had prepared Victoria and now it was time for Zara to come undone. She was so aroused it would be just the touch of his fingertips and that would set her off. Without a single look back, she left with one thing on her mind and it was not what was going to happen in the dining room.

Chapter 12

Having let go of the chair, Damion came around to where Victoria was standing. He could smell the lotion which he had chosen, like everything else, specifically for her. It mixed so well with her own chemistry that he was pleased there were no fragrant flowers to drown out the unique scent of Victoria. Itching to touch her even in the smallest of ways, he gently reached his hand out to draw her to the seat directly opposite his. Her skin was so soft and smooth; even though his imagination was running wild he had to keep it together through dinner. With his other hand, he pulled out the chair, which had a lower back than his; for reasons, she would realize soon enough.

Victoria was looking at him with a smirk on her face: what was that about, he wondered. Damion was sure she hadn't noticed the seat of the chair, as it was not like a normal one. In fact, there were not many things in this house that were considered normal. Knowing that she was without under garments however, he knew that she would feel everything. As he helped her to sit down, he saw the panels of her skirt fall across her thighs leaving him wanting more. Quickly he moved to his seat and focused on his dinner that would be out promptly; it gave him the time to calm down just a little bit. He was also highly aroused and in danger of completely failing at bringing her into this gently. Victoria was too stunned to say anything when she walked into the room. Damion was even better looking than she remembered from earlier that day and, as he walked closer, she could smell his cologne. God, he smelt fantastic, erotic in every way! The weird thought of just smelling his entire body brought a smirk to her mouth.

When he reached out and clasped her hand in his and brought her to the chair, she was reminded of how he was the perfect gentleman, pulling out her chair and all. As he walked to his seat, still no words had been said. It should have been awkward but it wasn't; in fact, it was as if this was a daily dinner ritual for her. She did admire how he looked in his dinner jacket and black trousers and, once he had sat down, she could see that his shirt was impossibly white. Her whites where never that white! How did he do that, she wondered? Then she quickly reminded herself that he had staff to deal with those kinds of things.

Her mind was wandering all over the place with all sorts of thoughts, like what was for dinner? What if she didn't like it? Could she say anything or just politely say she wasn't that hungry. Contemplating that, her stomach took that moment to comment on how hungry she actually was. Hopefully he didn't hear that as she would be mortified. Beginning to fidget, she reached for the napkin to place it in her lap. Only then did she hear him speak.

"You do not need to do that, Eric will take care of that for you. I do hope you enjoy what chef has prepared for us."

How could she not? She loved food and the fact that she didn't have to prepare it or clean up after it was definitely a huge bonus.

She responded with, "I am positive I will love it, whatever your chef prepared. I'm very easy to please".

Totally embarrassed having said that and hoping that he knew she meant easily pleased with food, she looked down at her hands and folded them neatly in her lap. Once she had sat down the panels of her skirt had slide down to the sides of her thighs leaving her legs bare. Up to that point, she hadn't noticed the chill in the air. It wasn't unpleasant just not as warm as she had first thought. Her train of thought was interrupted when someone, she assumed Eric, placed a plate of food in front of her. This was going to be good she thought.

He couldn't help but watch her squirm with her proclamation of being easily pleased. He knew she was talking about food but he was pretty sure she also meant in other avenues as well. Avenues he was anxious to explore but before he could come back with some kind of response, Eric arrived with dinner. He knew it would be spectacular. Damion didn't employ just anyone; only the best would do for him and his chef was no different.

Watching her tentatively take a bite, Damion knew this was the correct meal. She even made the act of eating an erotic and enticing event. It was going to be difficult to stomach food before he could physically explore Victoria. Perhaps just a little food now and he could eat properly later. Oh yes, that's what he was going to have to do, so instead of savoring the fabulous meal he just enjoyed how Victoria was eating and clearly enjoying her meal while he sipped on his wine.

Looking down at her plate after having had her fill, Victoria couldn't bring herself to look at him. She was so happy and a bundle of nerves: it was most definitely nervous excitement. She had never felt so beautiful in her life. Perhaps it was the incredible pampering earlier or the amazing dress itself that gave her the sense of beauty. Red was not a color she usually wore; however, the way this dress molded to her figure was exquisite. The blood red color was such a contrast to her pale skin that it stood out even more. With her hair pined at the nape of her neck and her back exposed she should have felt vulnerable but she didn't.

Leaning forward, she felt the chill of the room caress her back. It made her shiver. The dress hugged her breasts and would not yield to her nipples, which had been erect from the moment of her bathing. They were so sensitive that any movement of the delicate fabric forced an involuntary tremor to run through her very being. She was in a constant state of what could be described as arousal. As she had never felt this before for such a prolonged period of time, it was causing her to stew in the raw and alien sensation. Closing her legs under the table was supposed to give some comfort but, alas, as her skin was void of the most private hair, it made the junction at the apex of her legs throb with excitement.

The chair seat was shaped in a subtle saddle formation. Her bottom was hugged by the shape and, if she rocked her hips forward, it allowed for pressure on her sex. This made her intake a breath and, unable to stop herself, she looked up from her plate at Damion. He was staring at her. His eyes were so intense again she felt helplessly caught in his gaze. Exhaling slowly and trying desperately to keep the warble out of her voice, she said,

"You really do have the most amazing chef. Dinner was exceptional. Thank you."

She hoped that he would say something, as dinner had been in totally silence other than the ambient music. The silence was a torture in itself. He didn't say anything at first but then replied,

"I'm glad you enjoyed your meal. Hopefully it was sufficient but not too filling? I'm partial to meat; however, if you would rather not eat meat, let me know and I shall make the necessary changes to the meal plan from here on out."

"No, as I said, it was delicious and not too much. In fact, I couldn't eat it all but I enjoyed every mouthful."

The idea of eating was difficult enough without trying to finish. Even the food was adding to Victoria's arousal. The way it felt in her mouth and the flavors that burst were so intense. The asparagus was cooked to perfection, as was the fillet mignon. The baby potatoes with fresh parsley were such a welcome flavor to the tongue that she could have eaten all of it. As it was, she was to ready to really finish everything. The red wine that Damion had chosen complimented the meal exceptionally well. Vicky knew very little about pairing wine with food but she did reap the benefit of expertise. Still caught in his gaze and hoping something would happen, she sat back in her chair while he leaned forward in his and placed his forearms on the

table. The anticipation was driving her crazy but before she had the time to ask anything, Damion said,

"So, as you are here by your own free will, I am to assume you are so far comfortable with what you have experienced thus far?

Not waiting for an answer, he continued,

"I want you to be perfectly clear in understanding that absolutely nothing happens here without me either knowing or orchestrating it. This is one of my homes and I am in complete control of everything."

Having said that, he leaned back watching for her reaction to what he had just said.

Vicky at first assumed as much but after a few seconds realized that he knew about the bathing, but how? Had he demanded it to happen that way? Opening her mouth to speak, she was about to ask when she remembered that he was right. She had decided to come here and, yes, so far there had been some unexpected things happen but she was embracing or trying to embrace these things. She definitely was feeling new things and she was so ready to touch him that if it meant keeping her questions to herself then that's what she would do for the time being. So, instead she closed her mouth and just nodded. Vicky noticed he seemed to be pleased with her response as he got up from the table and started towards her.

Damion knew she was thinking about what happened to her and he was pretty sure she wanted to know if he knew all of the details. If she had asked, he would have told her but she surprised him by not and just nodding. That was good: she really was a mystery. He couldn't stop himself from going to her. This was the moment when he could touch her. He had moved to stand behind her chair and in a gentle but firm voice said, "Remember, you agreed to seven days and to be open to new things, so as of right now that begins with me. I have watched you savor your meal. I love seeing the way you enjoy the wine slipping past your lips to embrace the flavor of it. Your entire body reacts to every little thing. When you sit forward, I can see your skin flush with color and you let out a small sigh. The dress you are wearing was made for your body: it accentuates every asset you have and watching the fabric caress your skin was a theatrical event. But know this, I have wanted you ever since I laid eyes on you in the café. I have wanted to see if what I do to you will have any kind of reaction, so let's see."

While saying this, he had cupped her breasts and was moving to the sides where he slipped his hands inside of the top of the dress to feel the skin with his hands. The instant he felt her skin, his cock was rock hard. She felt amazing. He used his index fingers to rub her nipples in a circular motion. The peaks were so taught, he wanted to rip the top off her dress and devour them right there. But knowing the wait would be worth it, he continued with his exploration. He was going to enjoy every moment with her.

She was taking shallow breaths and her skin was responding to his touch. He was sure that she would be wet that her dress would show it. But he had a plan that he had formulated and wanted to continue with it. The heat that was coming off of her skin was in contrast with the chill in the room. Damion himself was on fire. He had purposely not touched himself; he had abstained from that all too feral release that he needed every day just to stay level headed. He considered himself to be a bit out of the range of normal. Not just from his appetite of sex but also from the way he needed to have it in order to have the full release. He was able to climax like most men, by his own hand, but he still didn't always feel entirely fulfilled. Just being here and touching Victoria's breasts made him begin to feel that all too familiar sensation of control. That's what he needed, as over the years he had honed in on that. Never in his sexual life had he ever gotten off from someone else being in control: Damion didn't think that would ever be possible. But then again, he would have laughed if someone had told him a year ago that he would have feelings towards a woman in any other way than just as a play mate. Yet with Victoria, he most definitely did.

He was spending too much time teasing her breasts that he was sure they were getting painful to the touch; he knew that she had been aroused for quite some time, a few hours at least. Removing his hands from her chest, he gently pulled her chair back.

He noticed that her breathing changed with the removal of his hands on her skin. She began to calm down and take more steady breathes. Not that he was against that but, for right now, he wanted – no needed – her to be almost broken with want of that climax, even if she was unsure of what that was. And, he was the one to give it to her. Not quite yet but soon and then he was certain she would have the best sleep she had ever had.

Pulling her chair back so that she was far enough away from the table, he walked to her side to pull her into a standing position. He placed his hands on either side of her face and brought his lips to hers in the softest kiss he could manage. Barely making contact was the key. When he pulled away, he felt her move forward to continue the kiss. A broad smile broke across his face and right there he knew she wanted him as much as he did her even if she didn't know it.

Vicky couldn't believe what was happening, one minute he was talking to her about why she agreed to be there and the next his hands where inside her dress touching and caressing her nipples. It felt so good. Was it wrong? Should she be annoyed that he had done that? Or should she just go with it and see if what her heart was telling her to do was the right thing? The feeling that just his fingers created was intense and again she found herself wanting, no needing, more. Then, all too soon, he had removed his hands and was pulling her to a standing position.

Before she had time to think, his hands where on her face and his lips just brushed hers. Not wanting the kiss to end she leaned into it but, before she could continue, he had pulled away. Opening her eyes, she saw he was looking at her again with the most breathtaking smile she had ever seen on any face.

Vicky was on an emotional rollercoaster. She wanted to rip his clothes off and explore his body but then again, he had made it abundantly clear this was to be done his way. What could possibly happen now? She had to ask, but how? Anyway, she could think of just sounded absurd in her head. Shifting from one foot to the other, she looked back up at him. Even with high heels on, he was a few inches taller than her. And, as her thighs brushed together, she audibly sighed in frustration.

Damion heard her frustrated sigh and raised his eye brow all the while holding her face. Again, not touching her was not an option.

"By that sound, I am guessing that you require something? I can guess what it is but I want you to tell me. Can you?"

Shocked that she had made the sound out loud, Victoria didn't want to answer but something in his tone demanded it. It was in stark contrast to how he was holding her face, as if she was made of porcelain, which she most certainly was not, so she did just what he had demanded.

"I, I do not know what to do?" she said timidly.

"That is not what you want to ask, however, if that how you want to be then until you do ask we shall continue." Damion responded.

Sliding his hand down her face to her hand, he began walking towards his chair at the opposite side of the table and started saying,

"As you can see, this is not an ordinary dining room table. I had it custom made specifically for my requirements. One of which is to have the centerpiece be just that, in the center. I love to look at things while I eat: be it art or scenery or you now! This table allows me to have that; I can see all of you right from my chair."

Walking to the middle of the table, Damion unlocked a panel with his spare hand and up came what looked like a wooden block. While that was happening, two holes appeared in the table itself a little towards his chair. The block of wood had leather padding on it. What could that possibly be for, Vicky wondered? None of this was making sense; she looked confused and couldn't help saying,

"What is that for? Why are there holes in the table?"

She reached for the holes and, on closer examination, she realized that they were not actual holes but looked rather like slots that were angled. Clearly, Vicky was totally confused.

Damion was pleased she had even asked that much: it would be more interesting to see her reaction now that she was interested.

"Well, as I just said, I enjoy looking at things and tonight you are going to be my art on the table. These slots are where your feet will go so please take of your shoes. And the leather block you are looking at is where you shall sit. In fact, let me help you raise your foot up... there, I shall just slip them off one at a time. I am sure this might be a strange request but believe me when I say that this is not just for my pleasure but yours as well. I am sure you are wondering how; just let me show you. In time, all will be revealed." Lifting her foot, Damion took off her shoes one at a time. This was a strange situation but Vicky was going to go with it. The next thing she knew, he was lifting her onto the block. Surprisingly, it was very comfortable and not in the way of their plates, which had mysteriously vanished. Damion was now placing one foot into the grooves on either side of the table and gently laying her back to what she thought was the table but actually was a raised platform – a bit like you would see at a gym for lifting the bars with weights on. From the angle she was at, she was able to see Damion's chair perfectly and was wondering what was going to happen next.

Damion was enjoying the whole process of positioning her on the table. Even without being able to see all of her, she was beautiful. She looked quite comfortable lying back. Now he was about to tie her down: this would be another test to see. So far, she seemed to be enjoying it all.

Walking to the side of the table, Damion pulled up the strap that was connected to the table and strapped it around her left thigh under her dress which pulled her thigh out in a butterfly position. Watching for a reaction, Damion kept his eyes on her as he tightened the strap. Only then did she look at him directly, not with fear but rather what looked like anticipation. He walked around to the other side and did the same to the right leg. She followed his movements with her eyes but never saying anything. Strapping her hands in the same fashion as her thighs was quick but it was only when he moved to his seat and slipped the panels of the dress to either side of her legs that her breath caught in her throat. He was so locked into her reaction that he saw her pupils dilate.

The way she was laying gave him the ability to look at her most private of places and he could smell her arousal without even looking at it. He kept his eyes on hers, looking for any discomfort of which there was none. While keeping his eyes on hers, he sat down and felt the heat coming from between her thighs. He wanted nothing more than to taste her and feel her juices on his face. To take his nose and breathe her deep into his lungs, but he was waiting. Waiting for the right moment, this was coming very soon.

Vicky was tingling all over and felt incredibly exposed, she was fine with all of this until he moved the panels of her dress, and this allowed him to see that she wasn't wearing any panties. Not that he had looked but she knew he would. She tried to move but, as she was strapped down, she couldn't move at all. Not that it hurt in anyway; in fact, she was very comfortable. She was, however, open to him and that was both exciting and frightening. Breaking eye contact as she was embarrassed, she looked at the ceiling for the first time: it was beautiful, with what looked like waves cascading across it. Telling herself to concentrate on that helped her... right until she felt something warm caress her sex. To her astonishment, she realized it was his breath. She couldn't look so she closed her eyes and let her other senses take over.

Damion was done. He couldn't wait any longer so breathed her in and blew out a soft, long breath across her beautiful pussy. She was completely shaved to his specification, which only added to the sensitivity for her. She had possibly the most beautiful pussy he had ever seen, and he had seen many. With her legs splayed the way they were, her labia had exposed her inner lips, which Damion wanted to suck into his mouth. Just at the entrance of her vagina, he could see the clear fluid that he wanted to lap up. He knew her juice would taste amazing but he instead brought his finger to the swollen nub of her clitoris and began stroking it.

He could see her body begin to tighten and heard her sharp quick intake of breath. Without thought, he plunged his thumb into her beautifully tight vagina. Immediately, his thumb was welcomed with juice that he had to taste. He pulled his thumb out and sucked it clean. She did taste amazing: he wanted more and could no longer wait. He brought his mouth to her pussy and closed his lips around her clitoris. The feeling of it in his mouth made him moan with pleasure. His cock was painfully hard, trapped inside his trousers. Soon, he would have to let it out but for now he was content with sucking her into his mouth.

Victoria tried to move but was unable to: this was the point of the straps. Damion loved that she was there for him to do with what he wanted and right now he wanted to lap up her juices and feel her clit continue to get harder and harder. While sucking her clit, he pushed one finger into her sex and thrust a few times before adding another one. Her vagina walls where contracting around him and he could feel her building towards climax. Feeling this on his fingers, he knew that when it was time for his cock, the sensation would be earth shattering. Not wanting that to happen just yet, Damion pulled his fingers out and lifted his mouth off of her clitoris. Looking towards her face, he could see her chest rising and falling quickly and her mouth was open gasping for more air. Sitting back and licking his lips, he said,

"I just knew that you would taste incredible. I'm not sure that seven days will be enough. If I could bottle your flavor, I would be even richer than I am now. How are you feeling right now?" He was doing his very best to sound non-fazed but he actually was the opposite.

Trying very hard to bring herself back to earth, Vicky couldn't believe that he was talking to her like he was talking about the weather. She was a mess! Just a moment ago she was on the precipice of climax and now she had to have a conversation. Trying to formulate words was a problem. She wanted to come so badly but alas that was cut short. Hoping that once she answered him he would take her over the edge, she said,

"Ready."

That was all Vicky could muster right now but she hoped that was enough to satisfy his curiosity of her feelings as she wasn't sure how much more she could take without release. Having never been on display before, she was glad that only Damion could see her or rather hoped that was the case. She didn't think she was an exhibitionist so this was totally out of her comfort zone. That's what only having sex in bed would do for you, and not good sex at that. She had felt more emotion over the last few hours than she ever did during her brief relationship with her ex. Her breathing was coming back to normal so she opened her eyes and focused on the waves above her head. She couldn't bring herself to look at him. It was his turn for an answer so she asked, "How about you what are you feeling?"

"How am I feeling? Well, let's see. I have you right where I want you: you look beautiful as my center piece on the table. I would show you off for all to see but alas I am feeling very selfish when it comes to you. I do not want others to see you yet! So, as for how I am feeling that would be possessive. Not in the way you are thinking, do not be frightened I will not hurt you. You are a mystery to me and, as I like those, I am so very much looking forward to unraveling your mystery. You see, what I love about you is that your body not only reacts to my touch but also to what I say. You are so responsive that without even saying a word I can gauge your thoughts. This pleases me to no end. Does that answer your question?"

Quite satisfied he had answered her question, Damion ran his finger up her left leg and stopped short of her sex. He knew that he would have to sate her soon and when he did she would explode, just as he would. Had she not been aroused for so long, he would leave her there for hours, toying with her as he pleased. But this was only the first night and there were six more day and nights to go. Plus, he just couldn't keep his hands off of her; he wanted to touch her all of her. He wanted to run his hands up and down her entire body and the only way to do that was to have her up from the table. Not yet though... he would have her there for a little while longer, just long enough to finish his wine. Perhaps he would taste it from her body: would that make the wine sweeter? He would find out now.

Victoria was still confused. Did that answer her question? No, not really, it just created more. What did he mean by share her? Vicky only agreed to be with him for seven days and nights, she never said anything about being shared. As for him feeling possessive, that didn't frighten her. Strangely, she was excited about it. She didn't feel that he would hurt her so that was not an issue and being a mystery was not something she thought she was. Her life had been very predictable up until last week so, how was she a mystery, she didn't know.

Vicky knew that her body was extremely sensitive and that was something that she loved. Being able to climax was not something that she had problems with; in fact, she was very good at it herself and Damion had been the starring role in her fantasies for quite some time but only recently she had a name and face to go with the body. Just as she was going to respond verbally yet again he was touching her. Immediately her body was brought to attention. God, she was so frustrated and wanted to touch him but the bindings where preventing that from happening. She had to get out of this and, just as she was about to demand it, Vicky felt something cold and wet running down between her sex lips. Feeling that against her hot clitoris was exhilarating! It was running down her channel to her bottom and was pooling. Her nipples were once again two hard peaks fighting against the dress top needing to be free and her entire body shuddered. Before she could say or do anything else, she felt Damion's tongue lap up the cold fluid from her sex. It felt amazing. Whimpering with anguish, she hoped he would hear her plea and let her up. She moved the only things she could, which were her feet, twisting them back and forth in the slots. This could be construed as torture if it didn't feel so good.

He could see that she was thinking about what he had just said to her as an answer and figured that she was thinking of a retort but he had to have her, so pouring wine on her seemed like a winning situation. He could finish his wine and see if it really did make it taste sweeter by mixing it with her juices. As soon as the liquid touched her, her body tensed up and a whimper came out of her. With one long lick of his tongue, he concluded that he was right; the mixture of the wine and her juices was intoxicating. It was time to take this to the next level. Forget finishing the wine, Damion began to release her from the bindings and sat her up. Victoria was flushed and somewhat dazed; so, giving her a moment to gather herself, he shifted his stance and said, "There are some things that I just enjoy and wine is one of them. However, tasting that from you was a new experience for me and was quite delectable. I'm going to ask you again, what do you want? I know what I want but you will need to tell me what it is that you want right now!"

He wasn't touching her but Vicky could feel the power coming from him in waves. He wanted an answer and she so desperately wanted to give him that but she couldn't formulate words to tell him. She felt that if he touched her once more she would come unraveled. She wanted to touch him and taste him. She wanted to feel him all of him but could she say that? Did she have the right? She was to give over to new experiences: was not telling him what she wanted one of those or did he really want to know? So instead she asked,

"Do you really want to know or should I just enjoy what is happening so far?"

"Victoria, make no mistake that when I ask you a direct question I would like you to give me an answer. This is not a rhetorical conversation. Like I said, I know what I want and I believe I know what you want but I want you to tell me with your own words. I want to see your mouth move and hear the words come out of it. This is not about me dictating how things will be but more of me expanding what you think you know or do not know. For example, you have had sex before correct?"

"Yes."

"Well, I am just going to extend your knowledge of that. I am pretty sure that you only have had sex in a bed and, judging by your non-verbal answer, I am correct. I do things a little differently. I will not hurt you but I will push you further than you think you can go. Take this table, for instance, this is not vanilla in any shape of form. Do you know what vanilla means?"

"Only that it is a flavor of ice cream, but I'm guessing that is not the meaning we are talking about," Vicky said with a smile. She had no idea what vanilla meant but she was ready to find out.

"Okay, we will have a lesson soon but right now I want to know what you want. You still haven't answered it and I need to know that you can!"

Vicky had I want you, I want to feel you and taste you, on the tip of her tongue but as she had never been very good at verbally expressing herself, she had to say it in a different way. But how? The best she could come up with and hoped it would be enough for Damion to finish this off was:

"Yes, you are right I want the same as you do, I think. I want this with you. Does that answer work for you?" She said this with absolute conviction.

Damion was searching her eyes; he knew that she was struggling to answer him. What she did say was pretty much what he expected. Her face flushed with embarrassment, which was ironic considering the position she was just in and everything that had happened so far, but for some reason verbalizing seemed to be a problem. She had admitted she wanted him so that was a green light for him. In due course, she would have to do better with words but for tonight that was fine.

Nodding his head slowly, Damion helped her of the table to a standing position. He waited a moment for her to get her balance before walking out of the dining room towards

another part of the house. Although he was not taking her to his pride and joy, his play room, he was taking her to one of the many bedrooms that was equipped with some of the things he liked to use. Her bare feet hardly made any sound along the marbled floor and, had he not been holding her hand, Damion would not have known she was behind him. It startled him that he enjoyed holding her hand, feeling her skin touching his and he even wanted her to touch him. That was something that was completely new. The others never got to touch. Not because of anything other than he was in complete control and that was his way.

As they were moving down the hall, Vicky was looking around and was suitably impressed with the vastness of this home. There were paintings along one wall and the other wall was just glass. The view out of the windows would have been impressive had it been light out. You would have seen the gardens and the pool, which looked large enough to hold a large party, yet intimate enough to feel alone and safe. She loved to swim and hoped that she would be able to use it, considering she was going to be here for seven days. Vicky was so happy that he was satisfied with her answer and they were going somewhere else that she didn't notice he had stopped walking and had opened one of the doors along the wall. Once inside, Damion flicked a switch and low lighting illuminated the room.

Much like the room she was staying in, the bed was in the center of the room with enough space to comfortably walk around it. A chest of drawers was leaning against the far wall and along the wall to the right stood a vanity with a stool. Unlike her room, this was decorated in a much more contemporary fashion. The furniture was sleek and solid, more metal and sharp edges rather than deep rich woods and thick bedding. The bed itself was like hers as it was a four poster and softening the metal frame were billowing white linens that gently cascaded from the frame. With the ceiling fan on, the draft was gently moving the linens giving a very romantic feel to the stark room. Under her feet was a thick white rug that encompassed the bed, making the bed look like an island floating away on a slight breeze and her toes where hidden beneath the plush rug.

Damion was watching Victoria for a reaction to this particular room. Just by walking in you would see the furnishings being contemporary and minimal but if you look closer there were signs that this room was not what it seemed. The frame of the bed was re-enforced steel to with stand considerable weight and the white linens where more durable and sturdy than they looked. In fact, they were strong enough to suspend a woman larger than Victoria, not that it mattered. He was here in this room to see how she reacted to it. All of it was important; he needed to put her off balance so that he could break down the barrier that was stopping her from verbally expressing her desires. Yes, he could just barge through them; in fact, that is what he always did but this was different. He was not sure where this was going and that was very exciting to him. His play world was always black and white but with Victoria, for the first time, there were splashes of color.

She was looking around the room with appreciation in her eyes. Damion had already figured out that she loved the arts, whether it was paintings or architecture, and this room was not like any others. He had tried to make sure that all the bedrooms were different. His own, of course, was his favorite. He would take her there tomorrow night but tonight it was to be in this room. He had to have her, to be inside of her, and this was one of the less provocative rooms that he had here. Pulling her to the side of the bed and with the back of her legs touching it, he gently raised his hand to the center of her chest and pushed her until she sat down. Tonight, was about releasing the pressure that had been built up throughout the day and right now was building again.

Victoria had taken in the room and the furnishing: this room was minimal in its appearance. And once Damion had taken her to the bed, she couldn't care less what was in it. Her body was on fire with need and was about to combust at any moment. She was now sitting on the bed looking up at him. As that was happening, he was removing his tie and jacket, not once looking away from her eyes. Victoria couldn't look away but she yearned to touch him, to help him. She was in such need of his contact that, before she could stop herself, she was reaching up to hold his hands. He didn't say a word just placed them at her sides and continued to undress out of his shirt.

Damion knew what she wanted, she wanted to touch him, and in due time that would happen but right now he had to have her. Having removed his jacket, tie and shirt, he made her stand so he could pull the dress off of her shoulders and down her body. The dress would pool at her feet. What he wasn't ready for was just how beautiful her skin was up close. Once the shoulders were free of the dress, he purposely dragged the top across her hard nipples making them bend and straighten at his will. Bending over, he flicked his tongue over one and then the other, nipping and sucking with gentle determination to control her gasps of pleasure. Smiling, he breathed out across them and dropped the dress. The natural weight of it pulled it from her body. Damion inhaled and could smell the lotion on her skin along with her arousal. Every woman had her own unique scent and he definitely was enjoying hers. Tomorrow he would have her aroused then make her give him her panties so he could breathe in her fragrance while watching her reaction. But tonight, he was going to have her.

She was still standing so he had her lay on her back, gently manipulating her body to be in the center of the bed. Once that was accomplished, he pulled his belt off and undressed until nothing was between their skins.

She was warm to touch and he was on fire. Not talking to her right now, it was all he could do to not come prematurely. Bending her knees towards her chest then out to the side, he was able to see just how in need she was. Her beautiful pussy was glistening with her juices and possessively he leaned his face down to breathe in and taste once again the magnificent flavor that was Victoria. Becoming drunk on her was easy to do and in no way fulfilling; he couldn't imagine ever being fulfilled, he would always need more. But, he was thinking about tonight. With that in mind, he pulled back to see her swollen clitoris and labia inviting him.

"I know what you want; you have shared it as well as you can for now but, know this, I am taking you right now. I have you all over my face, your juices are dripping down my chin, and your body is telling me more of what you want than your mouth did. This will change, not now but it will. I demand that. I want you to feel me: open your eyes and watch as I penetrate you with my hard cock."

With that said, he did just that: there was no need for lubrication and, at some point, he had donned a condom from somewhere that she couldn't explain. Vicky was so captivated by the command in his voice that she immediately did as he requested. He was big much bigger than her ex and she was slightly unsure how she would accommodate his size. Looking into his eyes, she pleaded with him and he answered,

"Do not fear, you were made to fit me."

Sliding into her, he could feel just how tight she actually was. The pleasures of the vice-like grip was almost enough to send him over the edge and, had it not been for his incredible control to maintain just that, he would have come at that moment. He had said that she was made to fit him and he meant that, only he was to have this. He didn't want to think about any other male being here before him or after.

Ridding the waves of increasing pleasure, Vicky was struck by how well he filled her. She had been certain that he wouldn't fit but he had said that as she was made just for him, was that true? She was so relieved that he was inside of her, she wasn't sure how much more teasing, if any, she could take as she could feel the buildup of her release. It wasn't a slow build, it was fast – almost too fast. She didn't want to end just yet but was tumbling out of her control. Whimpers of pleasure were escaping her mouth and soon it would be too late to stop. Just as she was reaching the point of no return, he stopped moving. She had inadvertently closed her eyes so immediately she opened them and looked at Damion.

"I told you to look at me, your pleasures are mine to keep. Only when you follow my instruction will you get what you want, what I want. I want to see your eyes: the way they change color with each moment of ecstasy as I slowly build you up to the end and feel me moving inside your tight drenched pussy."

And she did. She could feel him inside her, moving slowly at first then faster until there was no way she could stop the climax from happening. And, just when that was happening, she felt him swell inside her and command her to come along with him.

"Come now, with me." With that, he felt her tighten around his swollen cock and strangle his seed out of him. It was the most exquisite feeling he had ever had.

His orgasm had never been that intense. Resting his head between her breasts, he felt her heart racing with the after waves of orgasm and knew that she was done for the night. Her breathing became more controlled and her skin began to cool. Withdrawing from her pussy was not something he wanted to do but, as he knew just how pent up she had been all day, he would let her rest until tomorrow.

She didn't think she could speak after that so she closed her eyes and just enjoyed the feeling of what had just transpired. Tiny fireworks where rocketing off all over her body. With Damion resting his head on her chest, she had never felt so content before. Was this what it was supposed to feel like? She started to feel a chill wrap around her body as he withdrew from her pussy and more shockwaves settled through her. To her dismay, she was overcome with fatigue. She wanted to talk to him but couldn't keep her eyes open. Feeling something warm and soft lay across her body, she began to drift. "Only for a moment," she told herself but before she could finish that thought she had fallen fast asleep.

Chapter 13

Having covered Victoria with the soft blanket from the end of the bed, Damion just stood there watching her. The way in which her breathing became deeper as she slept was hypnotic, as was the rise and fall of her chest. He was stark naked, without a care in the world, but his mind was a jumble of thoughts and emotions. He really did mean what he had said about not sharing her or thinking about anyone before or after him, which was so completely out of the ordinary for him. Damion found that he was having feelings for her, ones that he was not ready to deal with. In fact, emotion was not something that came easily for him. He'd had a perfectly loving childhood but, as he came into adulthood, he had managed to put emotions into a box and store them away. Yes, he had strong feelings about things, especially if it was work related or tested his firm belief in loyalty, but not for women that he played with.

Standing there, watching her sleep, he shook his head to try and clear the feelings. He tried telling himself that this was just because of the orgasm... the afterglow of feeling... the release... but he knew he was lying to himself. This was more, so much more. He was feeling the cool air surround his moist body, which he had created from his need to have her. He decided as much as it pained him to leave Victoria he needed to shower.

Damion only showered in his master bathroom. It was his most private area, one that he had never shared with any of the playmates and only the housekeeper had been granted permission to clean it. This was where he could go and be totally at peace. Where he could let his guard down enough to completely relax, which was not something he felt he could do anywhere else in the world as someone was always trying to gain the upper hand over him. He really was a force to be reckoned with when it came to business.

He took one last look at her beautiful face and body that was covered with the blanket. He considered uncovering her and gazing upon her incredible body, but she looked so peaceful that the thought of interrupting that made him walk out of the room and close the door as quietly as possible. What was happening to him? What and why was he having these feelings? He didn't know but he had to figure this out or this week would fail before it really ever began!

The moment Damion felt the hot jets of water cascade down his body he had the overwhelming feeling of sheer exhaustion. Showering quickly, he would figure everything out in the morning when his head was clearer. Dragging his body to bed, he fell into a deep slumber.

Chapter 14

Victoria woke with a start! She sat up so quickly that she became a little disoriented and it took her a few moments to remember the night before. She lay back down as the memories of last night came back vividly. Not that it was a bad thing – on the contrary, it was more that the night had been everything and more than Victoria had imagined it would be like with Damion.

The only thing missing was she couldn't remember touching him. And that was something that she really wanted to do; it was something she had dreamt about doing and needed to do for her own sanity. What would he feel like? What did his skin feel like under her fingers? Would it be as soft as it looked or would it be hard? She knew that certain areas were hard as she could feel that from the penetration last night but what about the rest of him? She racked her brain but nothing came to mind.

Sighing out loud, she looked up at the ceiling and realized that it was really bright in the room. Looking to the left, she could see there was nothing but windows, and outside the palm trees were gently swaying against the blue sky, which was a brilliant sight to see, and not a cloud was visible. Drawing her eyes from the sky, she saw plenty of seating surrounding the largest pool she had ever seen. It seemed to stretch on for miles with no end in sight. By getting up and walking to the windows, she could see that it was actually an infinity pool hence to no end to it. Her skin began to have goose bumps and only then did she realize that she was naked. Quickly looking around the room, she was relieved to be alone this time. Rubbing her hands up her arms, she looked to the bed for some kind of blanket or robe to cover herself up with but couldn't find anything that would work. So instead she climbed back into the warmth of the bed. And anyway, she was certain the door was locked and she was unable to get out so she waited for someone to come to her.

It didn't take long, maybe less than five minutes, before the door opened and Zara entered. Seeing her made Vicky's heart flutter. What was it about this lady that did this to her? Yes, she was beautiful and extremely attentive, but there was something more to it. Blushing at the memory of the previous day, Vicky was unsure what to say so instead waited for Zara to initiate conversation first.

Zara could see Victoria lying in bed. Obviously, she was chilled as the sheets were pulled up to her chin. mused, Zara walked over to the bed with the robe in her hand and said, "Good morning, I hope that you are feeing rested from your long day yesterday and that you are ready for this day to start?"

Even though it sounded like a question, it was said in more of a statement. Therefore, Vicky didn't need to answer instead she nodded her head slowly and waited. Zara didn't disappoint. She continued walking to the bed without a second thought or waiting for an answer. Once at the bed, she pulled the sheets from Vicky and gently grasped her hand to have her stand up.

Zara could feel the warmth of Victoria's skin and see the slow blush that was creeping up her body. Victoria's nipples darkened with desire and her breath became hitched. Laying the robe on the bed, Zara brought up her other hand and started running lazy circles around Victoria's areola on her right breast. Zara loved nothing more than teasing someone as beautiful and receptive as

121

the beauty standing before her. This was part of what she was to do with all of them but with Victoria it just seemed to come naturally. Bringing all the girls to that heightened sense was invigorating and exciting, but Zara was finding that she wanted to play with Victoria herself and was hoping that it would happen soon. It was, of course, up to Damion but with a bit of luck it would happen. As it was now, she was content with this.

Vicky was becoming increasingly excited and her nipples were peaking: the slow circles that Zara was drawing around them was torture. Maybe if she moved just a little, Zara's finger would accidently touch her nipple? Moving ever so slightly, Victoria tried her move but it seemed that Zara anticipated it and stayed to course she was on. Looking to Zara's mouth, Vicky saw a smirk at the corner of it, parting her mouth slightly. Vicky brought her tongue out to dampen her lips that had become dry.

Vicky couldn't help but watch Zara's face. Her eyes were watching her, which allowed Vicky to gaze upon her without being seen until Zara lifted her eyes to meet her own. There was something there that Vicky couldn't pin point. Before anything could be said, Zara released her grasp on Vicky and brought her other hand up to cup Vicky's other breast. Without any thought, Zara bent forward while watching Victoria and opened her lips around that nipple. The feeling of the tight taut nipple in her mouth brought a groan to her throat. She felt herself moisten between her legs and knew she had to stop now or it would not be possible to do so. Dragging her teeth across the tight peak, she heard Victoria gasp and felt the shudder through her body. osculating the nipple with her tongue to sooth it, Zara brought her head up to Victoria's and said, "You must be ready to freshen up and bathe, yes? Let us go and do that. Your clothes have been laid out for you for today and, judging by how you were looking out of the window, I believe them to be the correct attire. Come, follow me."

Vicky was lost in sensory overload and was blindly following Zara. Only when she moved the hair that had fallen into her eyes did she realize that she was wearing the robe. When did that happen? She didn't remember being dressed in it but, yes, she was in desperate need of the toilet and a shower, a cold one at that. She was also hungry. Smiling, she remembered that last night's activities had indeed made her hungry. Maybe she would see Damion at breakfast and there she could ask some questions. But right now, the shower sounded like a good start.

Before Vicky knew it, she was back in the room she had started in yesterday but, unlike then, in the bathroom there were all kinds of soaps, shampoo, conditioners and lotions. Once she had relieved herself, Zara came in and turned on the shower. It wasn't until Vicky was feeling the heat and pressure from the jets that she realized she was not alone in it. With her hair wet, she felt Zara lathering it with the most amazing-smelling shampoo she had ever smelt. It was the same as the soap from yesterday; it was relaxing her again allowing her to not to think about what was happening. With her hair thoroughly washed, Vicky was about to grab the soap when she felt Zara slip her hands around to the front of her body and start to wash her.

"I can wash myself you know, you don't have to do everything for me"

It was out of her mouth before she could even think about it. "Yes, I am aware that you can but, as you can gather and I have said before, it's part of what I do is to take care of your bathing and dressing. I find great pleasure in doing so and Damion requires it. This too is something you will have to embrace; just another step along your adventure."

All the while Zara was saying this, she was running her soapy hands around Victoria's breasts and down between her legs. Nothing was left without being cleansed from the night before. Zara rinsed Victoria off by gently turning her around to rinse of the soap and only at that point that was done did Zara step out of the shower. Knowing that her clothes were wet didn't faze her at all. In fact, it only heightened her own excitement knowing that Victoria would see how aroused she was herself. Helping Victoria out of the shower, Zara felt her look at her.

Vicky started to step out of the shower only to feel Zara help her. Once she was out, she was able to see that Zara had clearly gone into the shower with her clothes on as they were plastered to her body. The white spaghetti-strapped top and boy shorts were transparent from the water. Vicky was taken by how she could see Zara's nipples and what appeared to be pubic hair at the junction of her legs. Strangely, she thought that she would have been shaved bare like Victoria had been but she was interested in seeing for herself. Not thinking she could or would ask, she didn't, but perhaps she could file that in her "to play with" file.

Accepting the towel to dry herself, Vicky began the task of doing just that. Zara was drying her hair with another towel and every so often would brush her body up against Vicky's. This was exciting. Vicky could feel the heat from Zara's skin through the clothing that she wore – even though she didn't speak, Vicky could almost hear Zara moaning at the very least. Or was that just Vicky? She was having unusual feelings and thoughts. She should be uncomfortable with being nude in front of another woman... she should not be having thoughts about Zara sexually... but she was both fine and excited by these thoughts and having Zara touching her in anyway was producing nonverbal reactions such as moans. Reminding herself yet again that this was an adventure and to embrace new and uncomfortable situations, she just let what was happening happen.

Zara enjoyed feeling her wet skin against Victoria's and, as much as she could, was making that happen. Here she was in control, well kind of... Damion was always watching and, yes, he would be very pleased with all of this but in the end, he was the one to take all of the pleasures. It was not very often that Zara was allowed to take a pleasure; in fact, she couldn't remember ever doing it. With Victoria, she was more than eager to do so and hoped that it would transpire at some point. However, right now she needed to get Victoria dressed in today's attire.

Walking Victoria out into the bedroom and discarding the towels now that she was dry, Zara brought her to the bed and picked up the lotion from it. Every time she bathed in anyway, she was instructed to rub lotion over Victoria's body. Again, not a hardship: this didn't take very long and, judging by the noises that Victoria was making, she was enjoying the process as well.

With her body supple from lotion and smelling divine, Vicky was in a lovely place. The attention she was receiving was taking some getting used to but she was finding that it was easier to do that. She decided that Zara was her chamber maid. Well, she would have been if they lived in that period of time but she didn't remember reading anything about the mistress being aroused by the chamber maid. But, to be honest, it didn't matter, the premise was the same.

Finally finding her voice, she asked, "So, what is on the agenda for today? Will I be allowed to do anything I want? Can I go outside? I would really like to go to the pool that I saw earlier: is that a possibility?"

Without even looking up at Victoria, Zara said, "There is no agenda, as you put it, this is all about trying new things and experiences. You are able to go outside and enjoy the pool that you saw earlier this morning. The only thing that you must do is wear the clothes that are put out for you every day. Mr. Foster has chosen them specifically for you and it is part of your agreement. Do not worry, he wouldn't see you in anything but the finest of clothing. You are very lucky to be of such importance to him. He does not allow that often, if ever!"

Zara said this while gathering the clothing for today that she had laid on the bed before getting Victoria earlier. Today, she was to wear the bikini and coverall that would only provide mental cover rather than actual cover. The bikini was made of the finest fabric that one could buy only at the expensive boutiques and, like everything else, was custom made. This one was the color of the Caribbean Sea a light blue with just a hint of green. There was no lining to it but once on, it formed perfectly to the body. It was made up of three triangles, the usual shape to a bikini: the difference, apart from the cost and material, was that they were very small triangles. In fact, they barely covered anything and that was the point. The sides of the bottoms had string ties that were not for decoration, they did actually undo with one pull of the string.

Again, they were made of the best material so as to not mark Victoria's skin. That was something that Damion might or might not do himself if he chose to, but if Zara knew him as well as she thought she did, she knew that there would be lovely marks placed there with intent. It was just a matter of whether or not Victoria could handle that side of him. Ultimately, that was not up to Zara and not something for her to worry about – sometimes she helped Damion but Victoria was special.

Once Zara had dressed Victoria, she placed the cover up (that was completely see through) over her and floated around her as she walked. She truly was a vision of beauty. Taking her to the kitchen for some breakfast was like watching a moving or a living piece of art. Being here for this long had changed almost everything about Zara and one of the benefits was the totally appreciation for the human form; whether it be male or female. To get to the kitchen meant walking past the foyer and the round table with the bell on it. She had seen Victoria look at it the day before but she didn't ask about it and hoped that would be the same today. It was not up to her to tell anyone about it and Zara most definitely didn't want to explain what it was and what the meaning of it was. Moving at a quicker pace and looking over her shoulder to Victoria, she said, "Come, we are away to the kitchen for breakfast before you venture outside. What do normally have for the first meal of the day?"

Noticing that their leisurely walk was swifter than expected, Victoria almost stumbled. Catching herself before that could happen, she was able to see the round table with the antique bell on it. It really was beautiful – there must be an amazing story behind that piece. She was curious and was about to ask about it when she heard Zara asking her about her breakfast habits. A bit odd, but she reminded herself that she didn't know these people so why should they know her eating habits. So, she answered, "Um, normally I just have hot tea and a glass of water right when I get up and then, about half an hour after that, I will eat something small, like a yogurt or a bagel. It really just depends on my mood that morning. How about you? What do you eat for breakfast?" she asked, genuinely interested.

Zara thought for a moment then answered, "This is not about me but, I too am not one to eat heavily in the morning. A hot drink is something I enjoy. Sybil will have what you are looking for so worry not."

Once Vicky was in the kitchen, there was a plethora of foods to choose from and many different hot drinks available. Vicky could smell the coffee but she was looking at the counter which was filled with pastries galore. To the right of that was a variety of cereal, much like you would see in a Hyatt for their continental breakfast. There was fresh orange juice, which was begging to be tasted and what looked like apple juice as well. Who was all this for? Surely not just her? For one thing, there was absolutely no way she could manage all of this. In fact, she was looking for the kettle to boil for her tea. But before she could, Zara handed her a white mug with piping hot water in it. She was just about to ask for the tea bags when Zara said,

"I know you must be overwhelmed with this spread. This is a normal breakfast for this house. There are many people here who will polish this off with ease. Just because you do not see them, do not think they are not around. Do not panic, they will not be able to see you either. Like I said before, we all have our tasks and they keep us very busy and hungry, as you can imagine. I know you were only able to see a small amount yesterday but know that the grounds here are vast, and maintaining them is quite the task. So is feeding everyone, so have what you want as little or as much as you chose and remember I can always get you something if you need it later on."

Victoria felt a small hiccup when hearing that there are so many people here and that she couldn't see them. It caused a little concern but that soon was diminished when Zara reassured her that they would not interfere with her either. Yes, she had only seen the entrance and a little of the pool in the back so judging by that she could understand why this place needed so many people to take care of it. She settled with her tea and a blueberry muffin and sat by the window. She then asked, "Will Damion be joining us? Um, it would be good to see him." She was shocked she had said this out loud and consequently began blushing profusely.

Zara only smiled and said, "Most likely not, Mr. Foster is terribly private and only comes out when he is ready and not before. Generally, he eats in his suite. Then goes to his office to work for hours on end. He is incredibly busy, but you never know. Please enjoy your food so we can get you set up outside for the day."

With that, Zara grabbed a cup of water and moved out of sight while Victoria finished her food. She didn't want Vicky to feel rushed and she had to get things ready outside anyway. The towel and suntan lotion were needed as it was going to be exceptionally hot today, especially as the Caribbean sun is incredibly strong and Victoria's skin was so fair that it could burn easily – and that would not work.

Vicky was looking out of the window as she was eating her food and taking in the view when she heard, "Good morning, I hope that you are well rested and ready to enjoy the splendor of the pool this morning?"

In shock, Vicky jumped and spilled her tea on the floor, luckily not on herself as it was still very hot. Completely embarrassed that she had done that, and that Damion was there talking to her, she fought with herself to not look at him but couldn't help it. She was so drawn to him that, even if she turned bright red, she had to see him. She didn't expect him here at all as Zara had suggested that he wouldn't come down.

He was just as handsome as he was last night. And thinking about him from last night, she did in fact turn bright red... but the smile that spread across her face could not have been hidden. She was embracing everything Zara had said in a small way, which was to take each moment as an adventure and, so far, she was enjoying them.

"Good morning to you. Yes, I did sleep very well thank you. How about you? When I woke, you were gone. I guess you had some business to take care of this morning?" she said with a little sass. It was strange waking up and being alone, especially after what transpired the night before and she would really have liked to wake up next to him. Maybe it would happen yet but, for right now, she just wanted to run outside and decompress a little. Seeing him there in the kitchen, dressed in board shorts and a tight vintage T-shirt, got her hot and bothered again. The cool water from the pool should help her get under control. She had totally forgotten about the spilled tea and half eaten muffin until Damion bent down with a towel and dried up the spill.

Watching her spill her tea Damion was instantly on the defense to help her, but seeing that it missed her beautiful skin he gave an inward sigh of relief. Scolding one's self is both painful and unpleasant. He was very glad that she had not done such. She had also surprised him with her statement about him being gone this morning: she was quite direct about it and it gave him hope that she would be more direct in other areas. When she had looked at him, her skin blossomed with color instantly. There again, with that unconscious act, he was aroused. He had tried very hard to stay away from her this morning by doing his normal routine but that was not possible, he had to see her. He had to be in close proximity so to see for himself that she was real. That he hadn't dreamt her that she was actually here in his home. What was happening to him? Distracting himself with the mundane task of cleaning up the spill, he grabbed the tea towel and came over to where she was sitting, bent down and began mopping it up. Yes, he had staff to take care of such things but it gave him the excuse to be close to her. Not that he really needed it but for some reason he was slightly unsure of himself this morning. It was not something he found pleasant. He could smell her body lotion and feel the warmth coming off of her skin. If he wasn't careful, he would rush this and he was not sure that would be such a good idea. She had looked so beautiful and innocent sitting there getting ready to go to the pool and yet she looked ripe and ready to be plucked for his liking. Without touching her, which was incredibly difficult, he stood up and moved away. Only then did he answer her.

"Yes, I needed to make an overseas call for work and, with the time difference, that was the only time to do it. Now, have you finished your breakfast? Do you need a refill for your tea as most of it landed on the floor? Do not become upset with me... I am merely trying to be helpful. If you would like more, you can; this is not a one cup only kind of place, anything you would like I can get for you. That I can promise." With that said, he backed away from her so that he wouldn't touch her.

Vicky was watching him. He was so close when he bent down to clean up the mess she had made, it would have been so easy to touch him, to feel him under her fingers but she couldn't do it, she couldn't bring herself too. What was happening? Isn't that what she wanted to do? That was all she could think about since she woke up this morning? Maybe with him moving away was a good thing, perhaps this would give her some time to think. Yes, going outside would be best. She had lost her appetite once he had talked to her anyway.

"Yes, I'm done, I think I shall just grab a water and head out to the pool deck if that's alright with you", she said not with any sarcasm but with honest interest. She was watching him to see his reaction, hoping that he didn't think she was being rude as that is not what she was. She didn't like rudeness and hoped that she didn't portray it.

Seeing that Victoria was worried about how she just phrased that, Damion smiled knowing that he could answer this in two ways. Not wanting her to close down, he let it slide on how she had responded, knowing that he could use it to his advantage at a later date. Instead he said, "Yes, that is fine, please make good use of it as I don't seem to have the time."

"Um, you mean that you do not use the pool? Why? If you don't mind me asking. I would think that with all the privacy and the beautiful weather you would take advantage of it." She was surprised that he didn't use his own pool. If it was hers, she would be in it every day, perhaps multiple times.

"Sadly, no I do not. I should though as it really is just there. There are others that do use it though and maybe I will one of these days. I love to swim but I just can't seem to find the time. Maybe I am making excuses but, to be honest, I just never really think about it that much.

So, here, have this water and make sure that Zara applies suntan lotion, as the sun here is much stronger than the Floridian sun and you could get easily sun burnt, and then you would not be able to enjoy the rest of our time together." With that hanging in the air as to what they would do together, he walked out of the kitchen without a backward glance. He needed to find Zara to give her the instructions for today. It didn't take long; in fact, she was on her way back into to kitchen so he stopped her and said, "I know that Victoria is going to be out by the pool today but by no means is her skin to be sunburnt. Make sure that she has the necessary application of sunscreen. She is also still to be on the brink but not to go over the edge. I know you are interested in her so this shouldn't be too difficult. Perhaps soon you can have her, I will think about it but for now please attend to her needs." With that he walked away to his office. He had work to address and although he didn't want to, being him was not as easy as people would think. He couldn't remember the time he took an actual vacation. Perhaps he should soon.

Once Zara had watched Damion walk away to his office, she headed back into the kitchen, fully expecting Victoria to be still eating. She wasn't; in fact, she was heading towards her with a bottle of water in hand. Zara could see something in her eyes but, not wanting to press to much, she just said, "Ready? Come on then; let's get you settled for the day. Do you need any books or magazines or music? All of which we have."

"No, I think I will just try and soak in the heat from the sun. When I looked out the window this morning, I could see umbrellas so if I get to warm I could always sit under them."

They were having this conversation while walking to the door that led from the kitchen to the back deck. The pool was even more impressive once Vicky was outside. The decking itself was stone and warm against her toes, and the color was the same as tropical white sand, which made the blue of the water stand out even more. Looking out across the massive pool, you could see the ocean. This pool was clearly an infinity pool, which made sense with the colors as they ran into the ocean and surrounding sand. Even though the ocean was a fare distance, it was possible to imagine you could reach out and touch it. Whoever designed this was a master at their craft. The illusion was perfect. To the left and right of the pool were lounge chairs and, at the end closest to the house, were two daybeds with white canopies. All the furniture was covered in plush white cushions and pillows. Off to the right was a large rectangle table with enough seats to accommodate a small army. All in all, it was just exceptionally beautiful. Walking over to one of the lounge chairs, Vicky pulled the coverall up over her head and felt her hair tickle her back. Instantly, goose bumps appeared, it was not cold out here but the gentle sensation of the hair strands made her shiver.

"Are you cold? I can get you a blanket if you would like?" Zara said with sincere concern in her voice. Vicky just shook her head and said,

"No, not cold just felt like someone walked over my grave, my hair tickled me that's all."

Looking around, Vicky said, "Are there any towels?"

But before she could ask anything else, Zara had produced a very soft and thick towel... from where, Vicky had no idea but she was grateful. She didn't want to get the cushion on the lounge chair dirty or covered in sweat. Graciously accepting the towel, Vicky sat down and stared out, enjoying how the sun felt on her skin. The next thing she felt was Zara applying suntan lotion to her legs and further up. In fact, she applied it to her whole front area minus what skin lay beneath the bikini.

"Turn over so I can do your back please. Like Mr. Foster said the sun here is much stronger and you can be easily burnt," Zara said.

After the initial shock, Vicky did turn over and it felt cold against her skin. She did smell like a coconut, which was quite pleasant and fitting considering she was in the Caribbean.

Once Zara had finished, she left without a word knowing that she would be just out of sight. In about an hour, she could come back and reapply. Lunch would be served later at the covered table as to provide shelter from the heat of the day.

Feeling that Zara had left, Vicky decided to take a dip, that way she could dry off while sun bathing. It served a good purpose. Getting up and walking across the warmed stone, she gingerly tested the water with her foot at the shallow end where it was a beach entrance. Feeling it was still a little cold, she decided that the only way she would get in was by diving in.

Fortunately, it was very deep at the deep end, how deep she wasn't sure but deep enough that she wouldn't hurt herself. Once she was in, Vicky immediately felt better, more awake and certainly refreshed. The sun hadn't warmed it up yet so the water still had a cold bite to it. Treading water, she could feel her body cover in goose bumps. That's when she decided to get out and lie in the sun for a while. Well, at least until she was dry then she would get back in again. Looking around, Vicky could see that no one was nearby so she had a thought. She had never sun bathed naked before and had always wanted to do that and swim nude. Perhaps now was the time. This was an adventure after all... so with another quick glance and not seeing anyone, she took a deep breath and removed her top then the bottoms. She was nervous but felt exhilarated. The gentle breeze across her skin was like light fingertips caressing her, she liked it. Vicky couldn't help smiling as she lay down on her stomach first. Listening to the wind through the palm trees was lulling her into a light sleep so she went with it.

Little did she know that there were at least two sets of eyes that had been watching her since the moment she walked outside. Zara and Damion both independently were ecstatic that she had disrobed. Zara couldn't wait for the hour to be up so she could reapply more lotion as now there was more skin to cover. Obviously, not her beautiful pussy but that would be getting attention in another way, which she knew would be amazing. With that thought, she immediately became aroused and found herself bringing her fingers down into her shorts to feel her own juices.

Damion had been watching Victoria from his office, where he had a camera covering the pool deck. In fact, he had cameras all over his property. He could zoom in and see everything, and every place on his compound was under surveillance. He was not a paranoid man but he did believe in security for himself and also his property and thanks to P. he had it where ever he was.

Damion was fascinated by Victoria: the way she moved, and now with almost everything she was tentative. Watching Zara cover Victoria's skin with suntan lotion was both practical and a turn on, what man alive wouldn't be by watching two women touching each other. The fact that Zara was beautiful in her own way was a benefit. He had gotten lucky with her, and the fact that she had wanted to stay with him even after everything was his good fortune.

Once Zara had left, Damion was able to focus on Victoria and the way she surveyed her surroundings. It was endearing how she tested the water with her foot, he knew that the water was chilled this time of day. Damion himself was an avid swimmer and usually would do laps very early in the morning or very late at night. It was cathartic to him, as well as great exercise; as he needed to stay in shape for his playtime as well as his own piece of mind.

Watching Victoria move to the deep end of the pool which was twenty feet deep – a normal pool for a house would be around eight feet but, like most things, Damion wanted more. Plus, with the extra depth, if he wanted to try out new scuba equipment this depth would provide him the ability to do so in the safety and privacy of his own space. Victoria had taken to diving in, which was the most effective way to submerge quickly. She was now lying on her back with her eyes closed. She looked so peaceful. Zooming in, he could see that she was chilled as her nipples were visible through the bikini top. He had specifically chosen that one as it didn't have a liner in it and would put her on display when wet. It was doing its job perfectly.

Damion felt movement in his shorts and knew that he was getting hard, this seemed to be the norm when looking at, or being around Victoria. He too was in a constant state of arousal. This was another new occurrence, which was something he was unsure of. Could this be something that he could get used to or not? He had never felt anything like this with any of the others. Yes, Victoria was different but she was female after all and he should be able to control his own reactions towards the fairer species, that was something that he had always been able to control.

For as long as he could remember, he had always attracted the attention of women, be it when he was in middle school, all throughout high school and beyond. When he was in high school, it was not just his fellow students but he would get the attention from the female teachers as well. Some of his mother's friends had tried to get his attention sexually but he had refused their advances. He was not interested in the "Mrs. Robinsons" of his mother's circle. Damion, even then, had a much more particular taste in whom he liked to play with. He had known from a relatively young age that he wanted more than vanilla sex. He had found a pornographic magazine inside his father's closet and was fascinated with the poses the women were in, what they were lying on or tied to. Even at the ripe old age of 14, he felt something once he had had his first sexual encounter, which was fast and very run of the mill.

His partner then was older by two years and had been a camp counselor during a summer camp that he had attended for many a summer. She was very pretty and physically fit, all of them were there. There hadn't been much conversation, just a series of fumbled hands and mouths along with a quick bump and grind, with her back up against the closest wall and his shorts around his ankles. Not much emotion other than not to get caught, which kept them going with adrenaline. It was over before it had even started. After that fiasco, Damion found other ways to please himself and his father's magazines did the trick. This is when he realized what he liked. During his university years, he had managed to talk a few of his fellow lady friends into experiencing his particular taste in sexual positions. Not all were a fan but no one was ever hurt or left feeling used. Damion had the up-most respect for women but he cultivated his preference over time and before long the list had come to inception. That definitely had a snowball effect, which led him where he was today.

Watching Victoria, Damion saw her swim to the side of the pool and exit. She walked the short distance to where the lounge chair held her towel and she did something rather unusual. She looked around and, with a sly grin, reached behind her back and undid her bikini top. Damion was transfixed with what she would do next. To his delight and surprise, he watched her step out of her bikini bottoms and stretch her arms high above her head, allowing him the most exquisite view of her athletic, naked body.

Damion had not realized that he was holding his breath until he could feel the pulsing throb along his cock. He exhaled and zoomed the camera in for a better and closer look. Victoria was stretched like a house cat ready to catch a nap in the sun and, as her skin was chilled, her nipples were still standing firm. With the camera zoomed in, he was able to make out the goose bumps along her skin, and at that point he wanted to go to her. Before he could get up, Victoria lay face down on the lounge chair obscuring the frontal view.

At that moment, it was all he could do to not go to her. In fact, he busied himself with the file sitting in front of him to distract himself from what was going on by the pool. Checking the clock on the wall, he knew it would be at least forty-five minutes before Zara would reapply the sun tan lotion. This would give him the time to compose himself before going to her. He knew that this would be sooner rather than later and at that point he would be alone with her to take her to the next step. Closing his eyes, he thought about anything other than what he would be doing to her... this was going to be difficult.

Chapter 15

Vicky could feel the darkness before she could see it. This was odd. She had lain down on her front and, as she could see shadow through her eye lids, it was apparent that she had fallen into a deeper sleep than she thought she would, and also that she had turned over onto her back. There clearly was someone standing over her, was it a grounds man? Vicky was stunned still at that thought. She remembered being told that she would never see any staff unless they were specifically meant to be in her presence but what if one had stumbled across her in her naked glory and fancied a closer look?

Too afraid to open her eyes entirely, she opened them just a fraction and couldn't make out who it was, only that it was someone. Taking in small breaths and chastising herself for being so brazen to lie down nude, she was about to ask the person for a towel when the shadowed person spoke.

"If you plan on sunbathing in the nude then it would be better to be covered with a layer of sun tan lotion. You wouldn't want to be sun burnt, as the rest of your time here would not be any fun. Besides, with what Mr. Foster has in store for you, your body needs to be in pristine condition, and, as you have some areas of skin that clearly have never seen the sun, it is imperative that you give that some protection."

Vicky knew immediately that the shadow figure was Zara. She was pleasantly surprised and a little embarrassed. She was not embarrassed that it was Zara but that she had actually taken her clothes off to sunbathe. It was something that she had always wanted to do but had never had the courage or really the place to do it.

Before she could respond, she felt Zara applying the cool lotion to her skin, starting again with her lower legs and travelling north. As her fingers drew closer to the insides of Vicky's thighs, unconsciously she parted them allowing Zara more access to her skin. It didn't occur to her that now Zara was inches away from her pussy. Even though it was obvious that she was, it was not until she heard Zara moan out loud did it become a realization to Vicky. She tried to close her thighs to no avail as Zara had a firm but gentle grip on them. At that moment, Vicky's eyes flew wide open and she had to stop this or at least protest verbally.

"Please, I will just put my bikini back on, I don't know why I even took it off."

She was pleading frantically hoping that it didn't come out as her being pathetic. She genuinely wanted to re-clothe herself but at that same time there was something to the way in which Zara was applying the pressure to her thighs to continue to open, exposing all of her. Vicky's heart began to race and her breath became hitched, what was she to do? This was all about new things and adventures but could she do this? Was this all too much? Where was Damion? Was he going to leave her alone only with Zara and whatever was going on between them?

Damion was unable to focus on the file in front of him and causally glanced at his watch. It was time for Zara to continue with the careful caretaking of Victoria, he brought his eyes back to the monitors and immediately saw Zara doing just that. She was rubbing something on Victoria's legs and parting her thighs. Victoria was leaning on her elbows and her head had fallen back exposing her firm breasts pointing to the blue sky above. What a view that would have been from above, maybe he would have to figure out how to accomplish that angle he thought.

That was for later, right now he was transfixed with the scene on the monitor. Not being able to hear what was being said, but he could see that there was dialog between them and in Zara's eyes was longing. He knew that Zara wanted to play with Victoria: she had all but said it to him but he felt very possessive about Victoria. He didn't, at the moment, want to share her. He wanted all of her pleasures for himself and if that meant going out now then he was more than happy to oblige.

Rising from his office chair, the tightness in the front of his swim shorts was evident and could not be covered by the T- shirt he was wearing. He was finding that control was an effort but important. He didn't want to go to her with visible excitement; he needed to go out with a firm but relaxed appearance. He knew he wasn't but he needed to be in control; it was part of what did it for him. He knew there were others that used that control for pain primarily but for Damion the control was not about pain. Yes, in some play, pain did have its place and, with the others, they were aware of these elements, as it was plainly explained to each and every one of them. Some relished in it and those that did, Damion happily passed their names on to other people he knew that preferred that as their focus. But for Damion that was a secondary field of play, he was more into the absolute satisfaction of control. How everything he did was what led to the ultimate release of pleasure.

With that thought in mind, he did his very best to placate his arousal enough to go to Vicky. It was evident that being away from her was not advantageous to his body. He was going to have to speed up his plans for her, giving her as much space to acclimate was not working for him, or her it seemed. Having her kept on the brink of heightened arousal was art in its self but he was feeling greedy and wanted her now!

Having managed to gather his thoughts and calm his body, he left the confines of his office and headed to the pool deck. As he left, he stole one last glance at the monitor and he could see that Zara was ready to take the plunge into Victoria's pussy. He must to get to her. Zara would not overstep her directions but it was time to take her.

Vicky could only stare helplessly into Zara's eyes and hope that she had listened to her plea. As it was, her legs were spread and Zara was so close to her pussy she could feel her warm breath tickle it. Having no hair had made her so much more sensitive, just the slightest breath from Zara was exciting her. The battle in her head was intense. As embarrassed as she was to be lying on her back, propped on her elbows and legs spread, the thought of grabbing Zara by the head and guiding her face to her pussy was almost too much. She couldn't do it, nor could she move. Paralyzed with want, she felt something warm trickle down towards her bottom, and immediately felt the pulsing throb inside her channel.

Zara was ready, she wanted to taste Victoria so badly, but knew that was not the objective. It was evident that Victoria was getting close to coming and that was not what she was to do. Just the crest of it; that was her job.

Zara stole a look into Victoria's pussy and saw the juices running a trail down to her anus. It was such a beautiful and inviting sight to see; she wanted to lick that trail and taste her. Bringing her eyes to the origin of the juices, she could see that it was pulsating. It took tremendous amount of strength to not dive in. She was unbelievably aroused and knew that with just a quick touch to her own clit she would shatter in orgasmic bliss. Breathing in and out, it was all Zara could do to stop herself from doing what she really wanted, to caress Victoria's clitoris. It was a good thing too, as looking up to Victoria's face, she saw Damion approach from behind her. Judging by the expression on his face, he had watched everything as he always did. The look of determination on his face said it all: at that point, Zara had to leave, her job was done and within seconds Damion would be there. Zara pulled back and stood slowly knowing that her nipples where on display, standing taut and firm. The brush of the tank top was keeping her aroused as much as she could stand. Between her thighs, she could feel the slippery wetness gather and ready to overflow. Stretching her hands above her head, she sighed out loud and said,

"You are beautiful just as you are. There is no need to cover your body with clothing. I like that you decided to sunbath nude and this is the perfect place to do so. No one around to see you but, as I said before, it is very important to use sun screen, being sun burnt is not fun and can be very painful. Just lie here and relax, lunch will be served soon."

With that she walked away. She smiled knowing that she would find Phillippe and take care of herself and her husband; he was always ready to help.

Watching Zara disappear, Vicky let out the breath she had been holding. She was so aroused that she thought about touching herself but didn't as she was sure she would be caught by someone. Lying back down and bring her arms to cover her eyes, she closed her legs but quickly opened them again, moaning out loud as the intense arousal feeling was too much. Spreading her legs as wide as she possibly could, she dangled her feet off the sides of the lounge chair. She was so hot that she felt the need to dive in the cool waters of the pool.

Looking at the pool, she decided that she needed to catch her breath and get herself under control. She was too aroused and needed to calm down. Not getting dressed seemed like a really good idea and would take too much effort at the moment. With the hot sun kissing her skin, she began to regulate her breathing and her thoughts. She was none the wiser that, just out of sight behind her, Damion was watching her every move. Much like a leopard stalking his prey.

Damion had seen Zara look up and see him. She knew her place and he also had known she would not disappoint. Once Zara had left Victoria, comforting her with the words of not re-dressing, which she clearly had decided was a good idea, he knew that she would go and relieve the pressure that was built up between her legs by finding Phillippe to do so. He had made sure that they knew that was allowed and even expected – there was no point in having staff who were sexually frustrated as he needed them on their game at all times.

Now that Victoria's breathing had regulated, Damion walked a large circle so he could see her from her toes up. This gave him the vantage point of seeing her

147

spread legs and her glistening pussy. Just standing there, it was obvious to him that her arousal was not being tamed. Smiling, he liked that. He was going to use that to his advantage. Walking slowly, as not to startle her, he made his way round until he was standing at the foot end of where she was lying down with her arms covering her eyes. She was so beautiful, ready and waiting for him. As the sun was high, it would not betray him with his shadow. Instead, he spoke quietly and gently.

"You have had quite a morning already. I hope that the pool was refreshing and your nap was pleasant. No, don't be alarmed, and put your arms up over your head again. You really are totally unaware of how beautiful you are, aren't you?"

He watched Victoria open her mouth as if to answer…

"No, don't answer. This was rhetorical as I know the answer already. Seeing you spread and ready does things to me, makes me want to do things you. Perhaps things you want me to do or perhaps things you would have never thought of. But right now, I want to taste the juice that is running its trail out of your pussy and down to your anus.

Breathe Victoria, I can see that you're so aroused by what Zara was doing to you, and do you know what that does to me? I will tell you, it excites me.

I didn't explain very much last night but I will tell you this; I will have all of your orgasms. I will be the one to relish in those moments and you will always know that I was the one to bring you to that point of release. You may be toyed with by others but the finale will always be mine.

I like control Victoria and I have it always, as you can see, on the outside. But, you wouldn't know what this sight does to me inside. I am able to control my senses but, on the inside, I am ready to claim you. I am not sure if the little time we have together will ever be enough. But, as for right now, I am going to taste you. Are you ready? Again, that was rhetorical..."

Damion kneeled down and gently pulled her down towards the end of the lounge chair. With her knees over his arms, he bent his head and breathed in the heady scent of her. It was hard to describe, other than intoxicating. The sounds that where escaping her lips were music to his ears. He brought his tongue up from the point where her juices were pooling and brushed it all the way to her clitoris.

As soon as her juices touched his tongue, he was lost. The flavor was incredible. The sweet honey danced across his taste buds in sheer delight. Bringing his tongue down the origin of the juice, he penetrated the channel and scooped as much of her as he could with his tongue. Burrowing his nose into the folds of her lips and moaning, he caused a vibration on her clitoris., At that point, he had to stop as anymore would result in her coming. Not yet, there was more he wanted from her, more he wanted to do to her.

Vicky was just catching her breath when she heard his voice. Damion was talking to her and, judging by the proximity, he was close. Bringing her arms away from her face, she could see him. He had told her to put her arms up over her head and without hesitation she did just that. His voice was soft but his words where strong; his message was clear and she liked it. No, she loved it. When he talked about being toyed with by others, she should have been horrified but she was excited instead. And when he talked about what he wanted to do and that she might want him to do, she was glad he told her not to speak. She wasn't sure she could. Vicky had no idea what she wanted and she was drunk on his voice, the gentleness of it. She shivered when he said he liked control, should she have been afraid?

She wasn't; in fact, she felt the opposite: she was excited. Giving in to his every whim was what Vicky wanted. The journey he wanted to take her on, she was happy to go along willingly. Being told she wasn't allowed to speak excited her, and when he took control of her body and brought it to his mouth, she almost lost it at that moment. Vicky was so far gone that it would only take a few swipes of his tongue and she would be sailing on the waves of ecstasy. Vicky felt every crevice his tongue touched, and when it penetrated her, she felt the build. Riding this rollercoaster was exhilarating. Once the vibration started, the peak was almost there. But just as soon as he savagely took her, he stopped, leaving her on the precipice of exhilaration. Feeling jilted, Vicky found her voice.

"It's too much. I don't think I can take much more. I want to touch you and feel you inside of me again. I want, I want..." but she couldn't finish saying what she wanted. As she didn't know. Her breathing and her heartbeat where hammering at the same speed.

Damion looked up. He knew full well that she couldn't take much more, but there was a little room left to toy with her. She had spoken and had almost said it, said what she really wanted. Did she not say because she was afraid? No, that wasn't it. Perhaps she felt that she shouldn't say even though he had repeatedly told her last night to tell him. Again, no that was not it. Damion surmised it was the fact that she truly didn't know where to go from here. Her lack of experience shone out from her. Even though she was no virgin, she might as well have been. It was time to bring her inside to his Toy Room. Damion thought briefly it might be too soon but at this point he too was ready to see her in his bindings, to become one with the room.

"Come," that's all he said but with authority. Damion was done with vanilla, he wanted to share the many flavors with Victoria. He grabbed her hand and started walking around the pool to the closest door to his Toy Room. It was conveniently just off of his private suite, not that the playmates where aware of that. He still wasn't sure if he would share that with Victoria.

"Leave that. Someone will gather your bikini later and no one will see you right now. Look around; it is just you and I.I think I want you like this for the remainder of your stay; we shall see." All this he said while walking with purposed control.

Vicky was not sure about walking naked but, as she wasn't given much time to do anything about it, she just followed Damion's lead, physically and mentally. She quite liked not wearing anything, a lot probably had to do with her heightened sensations. She could feel the heat of the day on her skin and the breath of wind caress all of her. Touching her in places she would not have thought possible.

Chapter 16

They were walking back to the house but going in through a different door. This one was off the side of the pool, it blended seamlessly with the wall. The only thing that gave it away was it was the only area with no glass. Otherwise, you would never have seen it. Once through the door, Vicky was completely blind. It was so dark and even squinting didn't work.

"Give it a moment for your eyes to adjust to the lighting. This room is darker than most but it is lit. If you touch the wall, you will feel the soft texture of drapery, this has two purposes. One it deadens any sound and two it feels magnificent. They are heavy velvet curtains that surround the entire room. The only light you will see is if and when I want you too." Damion was lifting her hand so she could feel the velvet curtains. All of the senses were tested in here; sensory play was just that, play and very intense.

With Damion's guidance, Vicky could feel the texture of the velvet curtain. As he said it would be, it felt wonderful. Velvet has a certain feeling like no other. Gathering a handful, Vicky lifted it and sure enough it was extremely heavy. As her eyes adjusted to the dim lighting, she was able to make out that the color of the curtains was not what she expected. For some reason, she just assumed they would be deep red, but to her delight they were dark. So dark in fact that at first, she thought them to be black. Curious as the color, Vicky found her voice and asked the first question she had,

"What color are these? How big is this room and what is this room?" She was still focused on the curtains so she didn't think about what she had just asked. It just came out of her mouth as she was really taken by the velvet. Yes, Damion had given the very reasonable explanations for their use but why where they needed? What noise was he trying to deaden?

She kept touching the curtains as she liked the way they felt: cool under her fingers and so soft. Searching her memory for the last time she touched velvet, she couldn't remember ever feeling it like this. Was this high-end or a specific kind of velvet? All answers she really wanted to know. She had completely forgotten that she was standing there with not a stitch of clothing on.

Damion was watching in earnest how intensely Victoria was studying the velvet. It was obvious that sensory play would work very well with her – she was so engrossed in the touch and feel that she had forgotten that she was not wearing anything. He liked that a lot. It gave him ideas for things to do but perhaps not today. Today, he wanted her to come for him relatively quickly. Yes, he had to prolong it just a little and, of course, there would be a catch.

Damion loved this room. All of his homes across the globe had something similar to this room: they all had his toys and different ways that he could restrain or display the female at the time but he had never felt that any of them warranted the Ivy. Victoria would look amazing entangled in the Ivy. That was one of his personal favorites, just thinking about what that would look like had him hard and ready. He tried to clear his head of this image when he heard Victoria ask a question. He took a deep breath and answered as best he could without a waver in his voice, even though he was struggling with control of his own body.

"Midnight blue is the color. And, as far as the size of the room, it is big enough for what it is intended for. And, for your last question, that will become obvious shortly. Now that your eyes have adjusted, please look to the center of the room and you shall see a game in the middle. I am guessing that you know what it is." He waited for her to respond.

"Yes, I can see the game and it looks like chess or checkers judging by the checkered board itself. Are we going to play a game?" she asked with interest. All the while, she was absently stroking the velvet curtain and seemingly had still forgotten about her lack of clothing.

"Of sorts, it is in fact a chess board. Have you played before?"

"Um, yes a long time ago and I don't really remember the rules. Are you going to teach me?"

"Yes, I am; however, I have my own rules to go along with the actual rules of the game. Chess is a game of patience and strategy, which is one of the reasons I am taken with the game. It also can take a very long time to win so bearing that in mind, when we play today, it will be with one purpose: the first to take a pawn will, for today, win the game and depending on whom that will be will depend on what and how quickly things will happen. Come, as you can see there are also seats at the table. Please take your seat and we shall begin."

Damion walked Victoria over to the table and had her sit down. Once she was seated, he followed suit across from her. The temperature in this room was a comfortable seventy-two degrees and, with the heavy drapery keeping the warmth in, it really didn't need to be adjusted very often.

Watching for her reaction to what he was about to say, Damion started with the actual rules of chess.

"The idea of this game is to force your opponent into checkmate. Checkmate is accomplished by forcing the opponent's King into a position where it cannot move. Any move will, therefore, result in capture. At any point during the game, a player, in this case you or I, can concede defeat if victory is deemed impossible. As you can see, there are two different colors of the same pieces. The lay person would have them in wood and the difference would be the color choice of wood. Mine is not wood but the definition is still the same. I always play with the darkest side. Which allows you to go first. As you can see, it is already set up for playing. Are you ready or do you need more explanation?"

Not sure how to start, Vicky asked,

"How do you begin? You explained how to either win or lose but not how to start. What moves where?" She was interested in this, she had forgotten how to play. In school, she had dabbled but never really understood how to play, they all just made up their own rules. Her father had a chess set in his study but he wouldn't teacher her, or rather didn't teacher her; it just hadn't occurred to him or her to do so.

Paying very close attention, she waited for more explanation of the rules.

"Well, see the smaller pieces on the second row, they are called Pawns. They are what military personal would call the soldiers and are the front line. On the back row, you can see that standing tall and proud in the center of the board is the King with his very important Queen at his side, followed by the Bishop, Knight and finally the Rook. That piece is in the corner or on either end of the back row. Each piece has a significant move they can or cannot make; however, for today, I want you to only focus on the Pawns. Remember, they are the ones in the front row. The first one you move can move one or two squares to a vacant square directly in front of it but, once that is done, all the other Pawns, including that one, can only move one square at a time. Okay, are you ready now?" He said all of this while studying her for some recognition that she understood what he was saying. She had furrowed her brows in concentration, which was a good thing – this told him that she was really paying attention. Sitting back waiting for her to either start or respond, he smiled when she asked,

"Yes, I am ready but what are the stakes? You said that we are only going to focus on the Pawns for today and that a game can take a very long time but I want to know what we are playing for. As I'm naked already that obviously is not one of them, so what could they possibly be?" Victoria was becoming more comfortable in this state of undress and feeling a little bit bolder so she stared into his eyes waiting for a response. At this point, she truly didn't care what the stakes were as long as the ever-so-present itch of arousal was to be sated. She too sat back and waited for Damion to answer. Placing her hands in her lap she brushed against the top of her thighs. Even though it was her own touch, it made her open her legs for a reprisal. The waiting was a torture all of its own. This game could not start fast enough for her.

Before Damion could respond, another question fell from Victoria's lips.

"After I move my first Pawn in straight line, does that mean all Pawns have to follow suit? As in do they also have to only go in a straight line or can they go to a square that is diagonal?"

Distraction and focusing on the game was going to calm her body and her question was legit so she waited.

Damion was enjoying this more than he thought he would, seeing that she had inadvertently touched herself and brought her arousal back into play. He did enjoy watching her squirm but it was only fair that he answered her questions too. He began with,

"The stakes are this: whomever takes the first Pawn will win for today and that will decide how you come. As I have told you before, I live by control. Well, this does not change if you win. The only difference is what I will do with you if you do." Knowing that was not really an answer, he knew what she wanted, what she needed and he was very happy to oblige. However, only his way was going to make it happen. If she won then yes bringing her to that beautiful climax would not be as prolonged as he hoped but Damion was quite confident that he would be the one to win this game today. Sitting forward and placing his hands on either side of the board, he demanded from her only this:

"Let's begin."

Vicky not entirely pleased with the description of what the winner got, as it didn't really give her the freedom she wanted. She wanted to touch him or take him the way she wanted.

"That seems very unfair," she said. "If I win then surely I should be the one to decide what to do with you, not the other way around? Perhaps you should be the same as me, without clothing. That would at least make it a fair contest." She was feeling very bold and desperately wanted to see his body again. Just thinking about him sitting there in front of her without clothing and only a few feet away from her naked body was making her heat up from the inside out. Maybe this game wouldn't work if she couldn't find some of that control that Damion possessed and demonstrated all the time. Watching him, she could see the smile appear at the corner of his mouth but he made no attempt to disrobe. Instead, he said,

"Move your first Pawn, Victoria." With so much hunger in his voice, he demanded gently for her to begin. Damion was enjoying this side of her and, hoping that it would continue, he watched as her hand wavered over one of the Pawns as she made her first move. Without thought, he moved his Pawn too and the game began.

Neither of them spoke. Vicky had moved her piece two squares and he followed suit. When she moved another Pawn, he could see her fingers tremble but her face was focused. It was obvious she wanted to win but that was not to be. Not today anyway.

Feeling powerful for the first time in a long time, Vicky was enjoying the game. She moved her pieces across the board well but one fateful move ended her win, with Damion capturing one of her pieces. Excitement and annoyance raced through her body. Yes, she had wanted to win but what now? What was going to happen? She hadn't really seen much of this room and she really wasn't sure what it was for, other than it had a chess set and velvet curtains surrounding the walls. Not daring to look away from Damion, she sat still and heard him say,

"You are mine, I took the first Pawn so therefore I win today." Damion never raised his voice. He barely said it above a whisper but she had heard him. Her body reacted to how and what he had said with goose bumps appearing everywhere. The skin across her chest heated and the flush appeared giving her feelings away, there was no escaping; not that she wanted to anyway.

Damion knew it was to be. The entire duration of the game, he knew that he would win. What he didn't expect was how into the game Victoria was. She was focused, and with the right amount of practice, she would be an exceptional opponent. But not today. Today she was his and with that he stood up, walked around the table to her and pulled her up to a standing position.

"Come, I won therefore the stakes are mine, as are you. Your skin is telling me that you are actually fine with that, are you?" he asked sincerely.

For the briefest moment, Victoria thought about arguing her case as to why she should be able to lead but, as that was not what she really wanted, she instead said,

"Yes, yes I am." in a voice that was low and sultry.

Giving a slight nod, Damion walked Victoria over to one of his favorite toys, which he lovingly called the Ivy. As with the vine, this one had some of the same nuances. This would hold a person in place for as long as Damion permitted it. The arm and thigh clamps would bind Victoria, in this instance, in the position he wanted. This was something he very much wanted.

Having walked a short distance with Damion, Vicky was too excited to really pay too much attention to what was in the room. But Damion had stopped in front of a very strange-looking apparatus. There was a seat of sorts, so it was kind of like a chair, but coming from the back and extending out to the sides were arms with what Vicky could only describe as crab claws. As she looked down towards the seat, it looked very narrow and out to the sides of the seat were the same kind of crab claws but wider. The whole thing was connected to the wall somehow. Vicky looked at Damion slightly fearful. What was this thing for and did he expect her to be in it or on it?

Chapter 17

Damion was very focused on Victoria as he brought her to the Ivy. He could see fear and confusion all over her face.

Damion loved the Ivy., It would allow him to play with her in many ways. Having never seen one anywhere before, he had had this custom-made for him. He wanted a way to restrain a playmate without marking her body. He wanted a seat that would not hinder his ability to penetrate. He also wanted her thighs to be strained wide apart with her entirely on display. The arm clamps would hold around the biceps and push the playmates breasts forward and slightly up for the best angle. The whole mechanism was based in strong metal surrounded by foam and then velvet. The same velvet that was on the walls. The back piece was wide enough to offer support across the spine and along the erector spinae's (the muscles along the spine that connect with the latissimus dorsi, the very large back muscles). There are many muscles that make up the back and they need to be protected as much as possible. That is why the back had support but not too wide. The seat was only deep enough for perching on. Not actually for the whole bottom. It also could fold down so the playmate could stand with only her arms restrained. As the thigh and arm clamps would hold most of the weight from the playmate and, in this case, show Victoria off in the best way.

Damion began soothing her with an explanation of what it was she was looking at.

"This is the Ivy. From the moment I saw you this morning in the kitchen, I have wanted you in it. It will cause you no pain nor will it mark your skin. It is created to do just that. You said you trusted me and are willing to do anything. Is that still the case?" He asked seriously: he knew he was pushing her faster than she thought she was ready but he could no longer wait. It had to happen now.

Vicky was a little scared but, after he explained it, she wanted to know what it would feel like to be encased in the restrains.

"Yes, it is. It's just I've never seen anything like this. I'm not sure how this works but I'm very willing." She was trembling inside and her sex began throbbing thinking about the possibilities.

Before she could change her mind, she felt Damion pulling her forward and turning her so her back was flush against the cool velvet backing. He brought her left arm up and secured it into the clamp and then immediately did the same to the right. Damion then lifted her enough so that she was perched on what felt like the smallest seat ever. He then began restraining her thighs which brought them up so that she was totally exposed. Her hands were free and she could brush her fingers across her knees. If she was not so unbelievably turned on, she would have compared it to looking like an upside-down frog. For just a moment, she half expected him to cover her eyes but he didn't. Instead, he clarified,

"I want to see your eyes at all times. I want you to see that it is I who is doing these things to you and, most importantly, it is me who will take your orgasm. Your pussy is so full of your own juice's that it would only take but a moment for you to reach climax. I am not ready to give you that. You are the picture of perfection that I thought you would be and there are many things I could do to you right now, but we shall start with this." With that, he began by caressing the inside of her open thighs with one hand and plunged the other hand deep into her channel. He withdrew this hand and tasted the dripping nectar that ran down between his fingers. Moaning, he said,

"Your taste is sweet. I want to be reminded of you all day with it on my face. If the need arises, all I would need to do would take the tip of my tongue and lick my lip and I could taste you. That would surely make any boring business meeting far more interesting. Maybe I will

later but for now I want this: I want you to taste what I am tasting. Open your mouth." he commanded.

He plunged his fingers back into Victoria and brought them dripping to her mouth.

"Stick out your tongue. I want you to suck my fingers. I want you to lap all of your cream from the crevice between them." With his other hand, he began rubbing her clit, feeling the pebble tighten and harden with need. He ran his finger down to her channel plunged into it then brought that finger to her left nipple and coated it with her cream.

Vicky, helpless with need and restrained, did everything he asked. She tasted herself and found it not to be bad.(She had thought it might be but it wasn't.) When he started playing with her clit, she could feel the build, and the cream he gathered and coated on her nipple was making her fly higher. It wouldn't take long if he kept this up. Spread like this allowed her to feel his shorts brush her skin, and when he gathered both of her breasts in his large capable hands she could feel that he too was aroused. His hot, hard erection was straining against his shorts and was applying pressure to her clitoris. Vicky tried to wiggle her bottom hoping to capture his cock so he would fill her with it but to no avail. She couldn't move. Yes, that was the point of the restraints but she was getting so frustrated and needed him to fuck her.

Shocked by her blunt thought, she moaned louder than she thought. Damion said

"I told you that if I won it would be on my terms. I can feel your readiness and you can feel what you do to me. I am so hard but I want you first. I want you all over my face. I want to taste you with my tongue. I want to suck your nipples and claim your breast as mine. You make me much more possessive than I thought I ever would be. You have beguiled me with just who you are." With that, he sunk to his knees and plunged his face into her wet and waiting pussy. She tasted even better with his mouth than licking off his fingers. He could hear her moan out loud and feel her inner muscles contract against his tongue. Moaning himself, he plunged further into the delicious cup and drank as much as it would allow.

Vicky was so close to coming that her breath was shortening. Her skin was slick with beads of sweat and her womb was throbbing with intense pressure. Noises began escaping her mouth and she was pleading with him to come.

"Please, I'm ready, I need to come." She was at the precipice when Damion stopped what he was doing and stood up. His face was glistening with her juices and his eyes were dark as night, heady with desire. Damion could no longer prolong this play. He too wanted to come and, now he had her restrained in the Ivy, he couldn't wait. Pulling his shirt over his head and without taking his eyes off of her, he undid his shorts and kicked them to the side.

"Remember that I want you. I am taking pleasure from you because I want it, not because you asked, no, begged for it. I am very happy you did but right now I will have you." And with that he thrust his hot and heavy engorged tip of his cock into her dripping wet opening. Not wanting to hurt her, he let it happen slowly to start. But, once the crest of the head was swallowed by her cunt, he dove deep into her, the full length of his shaft. Pulling out slowly and relishing in the feeling, he thrust again, harder this time, building momentum. With her spread out for him, she was at his mercy.

Vicky could feel the head of his cock enter her and at once her body became on fire. Once all of his shaft was inside, she was full, full of his cock and full with pleasure. How was this to be? She was unable to touch him again and completely open to him, and she was so turned on that she could feel and hear her juices along his cock. It was a sound she had never heard before. It excited her; what was this feeling?

Damion began to pull out and thrust again, building speed. The noise was surprisingly adding to her arousal. The slapping of his balls against her ass was a feeling she had not had before and it was a sensation of its own. The build inside was almost to the top. She could no longer hold it and, with Damion moving so fast in and out, she came, shattering into a million pieces of sheer ecstasy.

Damion had felt her clench down on his cock and felt the exact moment that she came. As his own orgasm

165

was building, his scrotum tightened and he came with another thrust. Victoria milked the very last drop from his cock. Not wanting to pull out quickly, he rested his head on her forehead and they breathed in tandem, feeling her pulsate around his cock.

"You. Are. Incredible. I have never ever experienced anything like this with anyone before, ever." Damion whispered his admittance to her. He was lost in emotion and not in control of himself. He needed to be, and grudgingly pulled out of her. He was still rock hard and could probably have gone again but he needed and found that he wanted to tend to Victoria., She needed to be released from the Ivy. Very carefully he did just that. Undoing the clamps around her thighs and arms, he had her stand up slowly. Fortunately, this restraint didn't cut off circulation so that was not a problem, but being in that particular position did cause a wobble in the legs.

Vicky was not sure if she had just heard him correctly. Did he just say that he had never felt anything like that before? Because, if that was the case then they were both on the same page.

"Me either, but I guess you already know that." She said sheepishly. She was bone tired and her legs were beginning to cramp. Damion must have read her mind as, once he pulled out of her, he released her from the Ivy. It was not as frightening as she had first thought. In fact, she rather enjoyed it. Very slowly, Damion brought her to a standing position, allowing her to gather her wits. Vicky could feel Damion's cum running down the inside of her leg and was not sure what to do. She had never been so forthcoming with what she wanted and was quite shocked that she had asked him permission. No, begged to come.

What would he think? Maybe she should go, leave and not come back. There were so many thoughts going through her brain that it was hard to concentrate on what Damion was saying right now.

"Let's sit and I will get you something." Damion said as he walked her slowly back to the chair in front of the chess set. Once she was seated, he gathered a towel from one of the drawers in the bureau along the wall. There were many other things in there but this is what he needed now.

Vicky was happy to sit and not have to speak. She was not sure what she would say if he asked her anything. She was enjoying her climax and the tingling that was racing around her body so when Damion touched her with something soft between her legs, she nearly shot off the seat.

"It's just a towel, I am going to clean you up. You are so sensitive, I like that very much. So responsive. Hmm, yes very much." Damion was saying all the while cleaning his cum from between her thighs. He had marked her in the most possessive way. By coming inside of her. Thoughts of protection where immaterial at the moment and nothing was taking away the pleasure coursing through his body.

Vicky was feeling lightheaded and disorientated. She knew where she was and what had just transpired, but the current running through her body was heighted even now with every touch Damion made. Just the touch of the towel sent a shockwave through her.

Trying to focus and gather her thoughts, she shook her head, gently clearing away the cobwebs. Now Vicky was able to take a better look around the room. It was still dimly lit but she was able to make out distinguishing pieces of furniture. There was a tall dresser with many drawers standing against one of the walls. Next to that that was a bench with a black padded seat running the length of the bench. She had no idea what it could possibly be for but it reminded her of a bench that would be used for weight lifting. Next to that stood two very tall candelabras with large white candles protruding from them. That puzzled her. In fact, looking around was causing her to think of more questions that she wanted answered but, again, she couldn't verbalize them. Was this because she was still on the high of orgasm or was it that she was receding into herself?

Damion, still having the fire of orgasm coarse through his body, sat down now that he had cleaned her up. She was looking around the room with confusion written all over her face. Was she going to ask? Could she? Smiling and just waiting to see what she did next was wonderful, it was like watching a flower bloom for the first time. Her body was still very flushed from her orgasm and she didn't seem to notice that she was still unclothed. Yes, he preferred

her this way; maybe he would keep her like this all the time. How would she react to that? Being denied clothing? Would this be the thing to finally make her ask for things? He had seen a little of how she would ask, no beg as she did when she wanted to come and that had been wonderful. Recognizing that she could be molded into a perfect specimen but she was more. She was different from the others. Damion was never not aware of that and thus was treating her such. He would never have played chess with the other; he didn't care nor need them to be a part of the buildup. They knew what was expected of them and they didn't mind, well most of them didn't. The ones that did didn't stay long.

Glancing at the non-descript clock on the wall, he became aware of the time. It was well past the lunch hour, and he was famished. It had taken all of his will power to last as long as he had but he needed fuel and, judging by how Victoria looked, so did she. Damion had thrown his shirt and kicked of his shorts in the direction of the seat he was now seated on so here-dressed. He could not help but look at Victoria and want more, more all the time. She invoked this primal need and drive to have and hold onto. How was he ever going to be able to let her go in six days? That thought just seemed offensively intolerable.

"Come, as much as I enjoy you being at my will, I am ready for lunch. I've worked up quite an appetite; and you must be hungry as well." Damion said and waited for Victoria to respond. She was still in the headspace of the orgasm high. He had not taken her to the subspace yet; that was still to come. But for that, he needed her fed and very well rested as that would take a tremendous amount of trust and energy for her to feel relaxed enough to allow herself to ride the feeling of going under into the subspace. Just thinking about how and what he was going to do to get her there had erotic thoughts scrambling through his brain. Right now though, they needed to eat.

Vicky heard Damion talking to her and she brought her face to his. He was everything she ever wanted in a man. He was strong physically and clearly had strong intentions for what he wanted in life. Be it in what they had just done or in his line of work. This house and everything in it clearly was not bought off the shelf and he made her feel things even when she was not sure how to feel. This was way out of her league and the little questions of doubt crept into her mind. He could have anyone, any female, so why me? He had asked her a question or had it been a command? She was not sure, what she was sure of was her stomach was talking to her. Gathering her thoughts, she tried really hard to concentrate on what he had said. It was something about food. Being disorientated was making the process of deciphering what was said difficult. So, she answered in the only way possible at that moment. With a small nod of her head and hoped that was enough.

Damion watched Victoria respond with a nod of her head and smiled, he had done this to her. She was in this state because of him and what he had done with her. The way in which she responded to his every whim was intoxicating. Yes, he wanted to have her tell him what she wanted but, then again, he didn't want that. He liked that she gave herself to him. Everything always came back to the same thing. Control. Standing up, he walked the short distance to her and lifted her hand in his, pulling her out of the seat and walked to the door leading out to the pool deck. Once outside, the sun was high in the sky and the intense heat that met them was overwhelming at first. Damion felt Victoria resist but he kept moving knowing that she would follow.

Chapter 18

Vicky was blinded by the sun. While they had been inside, she had forgotten how strong the sun could be. And in that moment, she became very aware of her nakedness. Still holding Damion's hand as they walked around the pool, they passed the chair where her bikini was. She was leaning over to grab it when Damion said,

"No, no clothing. I want to see all of you while I eat lunch. You shall be under a shade, and let's be honest… the bikini really doesn't cover very much anyway. Also, I have seen and tasted you. Perhaps I will again at lunch...?" He was waiting and wanting her to challenge him on this, would she? Not allowing her to stop and pick the bikini up, he continued walking around past a table to where lunch would be had.

Vicky instantly was no longer able to enjoy her orgasm and was shocked not being able to cover up. It seemed unfair. Even though she would be protected from the harsh midday rays, she wanted to be clothed, even if it was scraps of material with not much coverage. It was a mental thing, she had never sat and eaten naked. Surely that was not hygienic?

Desperately, she wanted to argue and almost said as much but something kept her from doing so. What if someone else was there to bring them the food? Color crept to her face with embarrassment. She had to say something, anything. But she couldn't find the right words. In her head, she was saying. 'Don't be ridiculous! Of course, I need to wear something. You are, so why shouldn't I? What if others see me naked? I am not okay

171

with that.' But, instead of saying all this out loud, she just glared at him in the hope that her eyes said everything she wanted. As she would soon be sitting, she could fold her arms over her chest and cross her legs. Yes, that would do; he wouldn't be able to see very much. This made her smile a wicked smile and she didn't care if he could see it or not.

He could feel the resistance in her hand but held firm, only looking over his shoulder to gage the look on her face. Color had covered her beautiful face and then it looked as if she was about to say something but didn't. But her eyes where defiant and a wicked grin appeared on her lips. She was up to something, but what? This was going to be an interesting lunch.

Chapter 19

Zara had left Victoria in Damion's very capable hands; she had seen the desire in his eyes and decided to make a hasty retreat. She was burning up with own desire and needed to find Phillipe to release the pressure. Thankfully, he was not as far away as she initially thought. It turned out that he was just off the side of the house. Smiling a broad smile, she walked right up to him and without a word planted her lips onto his. Moaning at the instant electric connection, Zara pierced her tongue through Phillippe's lips.

It wasn't too much of a struggle as he freely opened up and took over. Phillipe was as much of a dominant force as Damion, the difference was he only had eyes for Zara. With that, he took control with her and only her. He did Damion's bidding and thoroughly enjoyed doing it but it was times like this, when he was with his wife, that what they had was all that he ever needed.

Lifting her up so that her legs were wrapped tightly around his waist, he began walking towards their quarters as they didn't live in the main house. That was Damion's domicile and

the separation was good for them. Phillipe and Zara were far enough away from the main house that it felt like their own home. Even though it was still on the property and in a moment's notice they could be back at the house.

Feeling Zara in his arms and clamped to him like a belt had his erection fighting for the heat of her sex. Phillippe picked up the pace to get to where he could lie her down. It was the need that drove him to do so. His cock was straining against his shorts, desperately wanting to feel the source of that heat.

Pushing open the door to their quarters, they were met with an instant rush of cool air from the air conditioning unit. Living in the tropics and not being locals, it was imperative to have such a luxury one that they were grateful for this amenity.

Feeling the coolness on their skin brought goose bumps immediately and, as they were both so sexually charged, it made the feeling even more intense. Phillipe looked down into Zara's eyes and said,

"Mon amour, tu es mon tout."

Zara, even though she was so hot and ready for Phillippe to be inside of her, couldn't help but feel the love and devotion that he had towards her by him just saying those six words in his native tongue. She had never felt so loved by anyone ever in her life in the way that Phillippe made her feel. She was not fluent in French by any means but she was trying very hard to learn and, with Damion's help, she was getting lessons on the side, so that one day soon she could surprise Phillippe with her words. Looking back into his eyes, she said,

"I love you... but if you don't take me to bed right now I might actually combust!"

Smiling down at his very horny wife, he gracefully and with purpose walked them to their room. This room was pretty basic but they didn't need a lot of things in it. They had their home elsewhere that was all them, with their special mementoes and trinkets. This place they called home while they were here with Damion. It was decorated in off-whites and pastels. The furniture, for the most part, was rattan and the bed had one of the most comfortable mattresses they had ever slept on. It was a four-poster bed with a canopy of billowing fabric draped around the wooden frame Caribbean style. Plush pillows covered the headboard and it had the thickest duvet to stave of the chill in the air.

Phillippe un-wrapped Zara from around his waist and ever-so gently placed her on their bed. Standing back for a moment just to take her all in, he was overcome with pride and joy knowing that she was his. His to do with as he wished – and the knowledge that she was always going to be with him made his heart expand with delight.

Zara was looking up at her sexy and strong husband, not only in the physical manner but also in his mental capacity. It would take a very strong man to be comfortable with his wife doing what she did and not feel jealous or discomfort. The life that they led was definitely not normal by society's standard's, but by theirs it was. Even the way they were introduced was anything but normal. But right now, looking up at him, she was unable to lie still. She was squirming and in awe of how she managed to find such a love as this.

Her need was tangible; the air around her was charged with her yearning., Unable to stop herself, Zara got to her knees and began taking of her top slowly. Inch by inch, she started with the straps, gently tugging them to free her arms. Her nipples were painfully erect, waiting for his touch beneath her top. And once her arms were free, she began with her tiny white shorts. They were the uniform but they were the sexiest thing she had ever worn: even though she was covered by cloth, she too was on display at any given moment and, with her excitement, it was in plain view by anyone to see. The dampness in her shorts was visible with lust and as she drew them down her legs, she felt it.

Looking at Phillippe, she could see that he too could see it and wanted it. She always wanted him anyway she could have him. Right now though, she wanted to show off for him... by doing as slow and as sensual a striptease as she could. It was clear that he didn't object to it...it was evident as her eyes were deliberately drawn to his groin, where his erection was straining against his white shorts, pushing against the seam.

Looking back to his face, she saw he was staring at her with desire and power, not saying anything but she felt it. She watched him and saw him take a step towards the bed, knowing

that her striptease was having the correct effect on him. Her pussy was swelling with the anticipation of his girth that the slow striptease was not fast enough. Quickly, she grabbed the bottom of the top and in one motion pulled it free above her head. Finally, Zara was on full display in the middle of their bed, on her knees and all it took was Phillipe to say,

"Come."

That one word held so much power, it was impossible to resist. Without a second thought, she crawled to the edge of the bed as he walked to it and waited. She didn't have to wait long before he touched her skin, the instant his fingers made contact with her skin, she saw and felt the deep connection. He only touched her shoulder but she knew what was to come.

Phillippe was thoroughly enjoying watching his wife perform her striptease but he was done waiting. He had known that he wanted her the moment he saw her walking towards him. He always wanted her anyway he could have her and now she was performing for him. Only him. She was the most beautiful creature he had ever laid eyes on and oozed sensuality. She had never looked at anyone the way she was looking at him right now and that was something he cherished at all times. Right now though, he needed to feel her, to taste her, to breathe her into his lungs. The connection he wanted was all consuming.

When he commanded her to come that was all it took for her to obey him. Watching her slink towards him, his penis was thickening with each move she made. Once she was in reach, he had to touch her. At first, he just stroked her shoulder, which enlisted an intake of breath from her lips. Watching her mouth, he saw her tongue lick her lips making them shine with moisture. Having seen her draw her shorts down her legs, he had witnessed her wetness; that was heaven to him. He needed more. With every caress he ever gave her, he filled so much love into it and he hoped she felt it. But now, he needed to be feral. The desire to be buried deep within her was overwhelming.

Standing over her with his hands on her shoulders, he was unable to stop the progression of his wandering hands; he had to feel her breasts in them. To feel the weight of them and bring her turgid nipple into his hot mouth. She was extremely receptive to his touch and he knew that she was very sensitive, especially in her heighted state of arousal.

Bringing his lips to enclose around the taut peek and adding a bite to it, he pulled it deeper into his mouth, which brought an increasing moan from his bride. She could not control her reactions at this point and was totally on autopilot. Releasing the now puckered nipple, he looked into her eyes and saw her drifting into subspace. Subspace was not achieved by many but those that could experience it felt things on such a deeper level that the overall feeling was fantastically freeing.

That is what he wanted, that is what she needed... only then did she completely give into him. This was the most significant act as it took absolute confidence and trust to allow yourself to be there. This is when the term submissive was at its most potently power point.

Phillippe relished in her trust and gave himself to her, only her. Her needs were as important as his but his desire was not dampened; in fact, it was heighted with her in subspace. Lying her down again, he said,

"That's it, only me, only us are here and I have you, you belong to me." He said this with absolute confidence and authority. His love for Zara was obvious but his control was substantial.

Bringing his hands back to her chest, he began teasing her areola. He wasn't actually touching her nipples, just feather touches around them to keep them hard. Then he brought his lips to one and inhaled it into his mouth. Rolling it around with his tongue, he moaned himself and brought his other hand to the juncture of her core. He could smell her arousal and in that moment needed to taste. Releasing her nipple, he moved to the bottom of the bed and grasped her ankles and deftly opened her up for him. Her legs spread wide for him and the view of her most intimate of places was shiny with her hunger. Crawling onto the bed between Zara's legs, he dove into her heat with a ferocity of carnal thirst. With one swipe of his tongue, he took her into his mouth and swallowed his bounty. Her taste was as unique as the woman she was. Sweet and spicy with a touch of vanilla. That was his wife: she loved vanilla but nothing about her was vanilla. With his hands pressed into her thighs, he opened her up even further and brought his tongue from her opening up to her hooded gem and clamped his teeth on her clitoris. She thrust her hips up and he obligingly accepted her in his mouth. Sucking with such force, he began to feel the build of orgasm within her as her thighs began to tremble. Knowing that all too soon she would fall over the precipice, he grudgingly released her clitoris from his mouth and positioned himself to enter her with his engorged cock.

Briefly allowing her respite as he disrobed, he commanded her to stay as she was with his eyes and to this she responded willingly. He was ready to have her wrapped around him. Without saying a word, he touched her heated clitoris with the tip of his penis and claimed it with his pre-cum.

Zara was fully aware of what was going on but was so cocooned by the subspace she couldn't move if she wanted to. Just Phillippe looking at her told her everything he wanted – he wanted her obedience and surrender. Both she would have given him willingly at any given moment. When the head of his cock made contact with her clitoris, she felt her body ignite. Phillippe smeared his pre-cum on her and blew on it: the sensation was in complete contrast to her heated skin that it made her jolt. Unable to form the words with her mouth, she hoped the urgency in her eyes told Phillippe that she wanted him to take her. To fill her with his cock and unite them as one.

Phillippe could see the want in her eyes and, when he blew gently on her clitoris, she bucked with desire. He had claimed her clitoris with his pre-cum but the ultimate ownership would be soon. He dragged his hot, hard cock over her clitoris and spread her labia with it to her open-soaked channel. As gently as he could, he entered her with just the tip, allowing for every fiber to embrace his member. He could feel Zara begin to stretch to accommodate his size; he was by no means enormous but he was not small either. The only thing that mattered was that he was what Zara wanted, anything else was immaterial. Taking his time was a torture all of its own, he wanted to ram into her and feel his balls slap against her ass checks. To hear the sound of the skin on skin, but this was an exercise in patience. One that he was enjoying.

Zara's skin became heated and brought a flush to her skin. With every centimeter he thrust more, feeling the welcomed tug of her inner muscles gripping him. The sensation was intoxicating... something he would never get used to. With one last, gentle thrust, he was embedded in her. He could feel her throb around his cock and her wetness dripping onto his balls. There was no need for lubrication but there was always some at the ready if needed. An audible moan escaped her mouth and he was overcome with need to move, he began withdrawing and penetrating, over and over, building up speed. His hands cupped her breasts and brought them together in the middle so he could take both her nipples into his mouth at once. Her cries began to increase and he released her breasts and lifted her legs to hook over his shoulders. This angle allowed for a deeper penetration. Increasing his speed and force, he could hear their skin slapping against one another. His body began to tighten and his own orgasm was getting closer. He knew Zara's body inside and out and could feel the walls of her vagina tighten around his cock and knew that her orgasm was close. Rising to his feet and in a crouching position, his tempo increasing, he thrust with so much force that the bed began to shake. No longer able to keep quiet, Zara was moaning in time with his tempo. Phillippe demanded,

"Come, come now! I want to feel you come on my cock as it is buried inside of you."

At that moment, Zara happily obliged to his demands. She came with such ferocity that stars exploded in her eyes and she was blinded with the feeling of release. Her vagina was convulsing around his shaft so hard she could feel the thick vein on the underside throb and his shaft swell filling her with every inch of him.

Phillippe, feeling Zara come on his cock, was unable to hold off any longer. With her inner muscles constricting around his shaft, he pumped into her one more time and came hard. He could feel his cum fly out of his dick and claim her in the most primal way. This was his and only his to do this too. She was marked with is seed. His climax was almost violent; he was a controlled man, but with Zara his release was impossible to contain.

With shouts of sheer pleasure, Zara heard Phillippe come inside of her. She felt the moment he shattered as his cum shot out of him with the feral need of ownership. She was his and needed claiming. Her body was electric and every movement brought joy and happiness. There was no one on this earth that could make her feel the way Phillippe did. Not even Damion could do that to her.

Phillippe was resting his head in the crook of her neck and kissing her while the last of his seed coated her insides. The love she had for this man was intense, she couldn't and wouldn't imagine what it would be like to not have him. She loved this. This feeling of her husband inside her still and feeling their hearts beat at the same elevated rhythm, chest to chest, skin on skin, their sweat mingling with each other and their juices intertwined.

As Phillippe's breath came back to him, his lips pressed against Zara's neck, gently kissing and nipping her. This was paradise, not the outside of this room but this, this moment spent with his wife, feeling her, all of her. He could still feel his semi-erect penis still inside of her and her channel coaxing every last drop of cum out of him.

"I love you. Forever, I will love you and then I will love you forever." Phillippe said and gently pulled out of her. Lying on his back, he brought her to him and, within moments, they both fell into a contented slumber.

Chapter 20

Walking around the pool deck, Damion did not slow down as he approached the table; he didn't stop his stride in fact he just kept on going. This was not where they were going to enjoy their lunch. He had a very different location in mind. A much more serene and secluded setting in mind. Not that the entire compound was not secluded, it was, but this had one of the best vantage points on the compound, with a spectacular view of the picture post card view of the beach.

Damion felt Victoria slow as they approached the table but, as he didn't stop walking, he tightened his grip on her hand and, looking over his shoulder at her, said,

"I have somewhere else in mind for lunch. This is not a place you have seen yet nor have you seen this view. It allows for full appreciation of many things, I'm sure you will agree." All this he said with a wink and a smile. The entire sentence was laced with innuendos – he knew she was smart enough to get them but, then again, would she engage in the playfulness of it? He would have to wait and see.

He felt her speed up a little, which meant he could release her hand a bit, but not enough to let go. He found that he really enjoyed the contact of their skin together, again something new. She certainly was bringing a lot of things for Damion to think and reflect on. Turning his face towards the direction they were walking in and not slowing down, he could see the corner of the deck and headed in that direction. Once there, he brought Victoria with him around the corner and waited for her to grasp what she could see. It didn't take long. He knew she would be in awe of the view of the beach but he was waiting to see how she would respond with their lunch table. In all honesty, he never cared enough about the others to do this or share this with them. They were silly girls in comparison, but he could only hope that Victoria could see it for what it was.

Vicky was a little confused. She thought that they were going to have lunch on the pool deck at the table under the shade but when Damion had passed that, she truly was confused. As they walked toward the end of the deck, there was nothing to see except vast green lawn that led to the beach but she couldn't see anything set up for lunch. No picnic area or another table and chairs under shade, nothing. Until… Damion brought her around the corner; there, recessed into the wall of the existing house, was a crescent-shaped indentation made of the same stone of the house. On the ground was a matching crescent shaped white cushion that surrounded a very low round glass table. On the top of the table was an array of plates, bowls and boards. All of which were brimming with food items of different textures, shapes and color. There were tall glasses filled with clear fluid and sliced lemon, which Vicky assumed was water, and next to those were empty wine glasses. Taking in the food, she could see that it was plentiful, but with no utensils visible, she figured this would be eaten by hand. She could not see any chairs to sit on and when she looked at Damion, she saw he was watching, no studying her. Unable to help herself, she asked,

"Do you expect me to eat this standing up?" It had not occurred to her that she would sit down.

184

Damion, seeing the confusion in her eyes, put her at ease with his response.

"You see the white cushion there on the ground? That is where you sit and where I will sit. This table is low for the purpose of sitting low. In many Arabic countries, it's how they eat all the time. The one major difference is that men and women do not eat together." With that said, he laid his hand gently on her back and firmly said.

"Sit"

Still a little shocked with how she was to eat, she couldn't help her brain from thinking "I'm not a dog". But, she obliged with his request, no it was more of a command. Sitting, however, was going to be a challenge. Feeling the light pressure of his hand across the small of her back, she looked down at the cushion and couldn't quite figure out how she could sit modestly. Perhaps if she sat with her back slightly turned to Damion then she would be less visible for this meal. Thinking this was the best option, she lowered herself to her knees and sat with her ankles crossed and her back facing Damion. Hopefully, lunch would not be a drawn-out experience and she would be free from this incredibly uncomfortable situation soon.

With that, she looked up to see a new person standing before them. In his hands, he was holding what appeared to be a glass bowl and in his other hand a pair of wooden tongs. What on earth could that be for, she wondered? The way in which he was standing, he was able to see all of her nakedness. She thought that turning her back to Damion would give her some modesty but she did not expect anyone else to be there at all. Oh my God, this was a nightmare that was not ending!

Bringing her arms up, she did her absolute best to cover her chest but no position did that! She tried every which way and nothing worked. She looked back to the man standing before her and realized that she could not see his eyes as they were hidden behind trendy wraparound sunglasses. The clothes he wore seemed to be of some kind of uniform: a navy-blue polo shirt and khaki Bermuda shorts were covering what appeared to be a fit body. His face was not telling much about his age but he was perhaps around her age, she couldn't tell. He had sun-bleached, shaggy hair that loosely hung around his shoulders and, as the table was clear, she could see that he was wearing flip flops. All in all, he looked comfortably casual, definitely something she was not at this time.

Giving up on covering herself, she leaned forward a little and sat staring at the table before her. She couldn't even bring herself to look at Damion, but she could feel his eyes watching her. She felt there was a tangible tie to him even if they were not physically touching.

Damion had enjoyed her discomfort in her display of sitting down. She had made such a meal of that already and they hadn't even started to enjoy the food that was laid out for them on the table. Simon had arrived during her performance and, as he was advised, no emotion was shown across his face. In fact, he looked perfectly disinterested even though Damion knew that was not the case. How could any breathing individual not be taken by Victoria? She had weaved some kind of magic spell over his entire camp and everyone was captivated by her.

Looking at Simon, he saw the water bowl and tongs in his hands and just waited a minute more before saying,

"Thank you, Simon, we will have the wash cloths now." Ashe said this, Simon removed one wash cloth from the bowl with the tongs, walked around to where he had access to Victoria and delivered one of them to her. The problem was she had her eyes cast down and didn't see it. It was not until she felt the hot water dripping down over her right breast did she gasp and look up to see where the water had come from. It was not hot enough to burn or even leave a mark but it was warm enough to startle her.

Still saying nothing, Simon just waited for her to accept the cloth. She did, but not before steeling a look at Damion quickly over her shoulder with annoyance. Damion was unable to suppress his delight in her reaction, what would it take for her to admit and say out loud how much this entire situation was not comfortable for her? What would be the point of no return? He surmised it would not be with the cloth– perhaps it would be with the lunch itself or could it be what was to come later? He didn't blatantly smile but his eyes were laughing, only she was not looking at him so therefore couldn't see the joy she was giving him in her defiance.

Damion watched as she accepted the wash cloth and turned her body to face the table. Now she was no longer on an angle, he was able to see that, with the combination of the water and the breeze, her right nipple was pebbled and her left one was coming up. They were the perfect rose petal nubs that he had ever seen. The desire to take them into his mouth was just about impossible to restrain from. But he had to. Control, which was what was going on here. However much his absolute desire was to sweep the contents of the table off and place her on it to feast from, he had to control that feeling, that need.

She too had control, so much that she didn't speak her mind, but her own body gave her away every time. The shades of color that encompassed her skin. And her eyes, those eyes were unable to lie. He loved that; loved that he could get such a reaction to something as simple as a wash cloth to clean her hands. Granted, this was not how she imagined being given one, he was absolutely positive that she had never been seated outside naked at a table like this ever before in her life. He could probably guess that she had never sat at a table like this before either. She would only be used to chairs and a table at regular height. But this was all about a new journey and new experiences, this would definitely be described as one. Simon had walked around to Damion and given the wash cloth to him. As he was cleaning his hands with it, he looked over to see that Victoria was doing the same. At least she knew what it was for – he hated having to explain to some of the women he was with what the purpose of the wash cloth was.

Once finished with the wash cloth, Damion gave it back to Simon, who then returned to Victoria's side and retrieved hers too. With that in hand, he disappeared as quickly and quietly he had arrived. Yes, Simon was going to work out perfectly, Damion thought, perhaps more duties might be in order. He would need to speak with P. soon for that.

Looking at Victoria again, he could see she was staring at the table of food and absently licking her lips. That was so hot and immediately his erection stood to attention again. Nothing more uncomfortable than an erection straining against your shorts and being unable to adjust yourself, as the position you are sitting in doesn't allow for it. It would take a lot of deep breathing and trying desperately to think about anything else but the gorgeous beauty sitting beside him. Clearing his throat, he reached across the table to the bottle of white wine and said,

"Care for some wine? It's white and very fruity; it will go nicely with our lunch."

He waited for her response as he would pour hers first – ladies before gents, he did have manners, even if no one thought he did. He just didn't need to have any with the playmates.

Vicky would love a glass of wine: it could and would take the edge of how she was feeling. She couldn't believe anyone was there with them – she thought it was just going to be them alone. She had heard Damion call the man Simon. Simon hadn't spoken one word to her but she felt embarrassed being on display for him to see. She hadn't seen him anywhere before. What did he do? Who was he? Where did he come from? All questions to be answered but right now she wanted wine.

"Yes, I would like that very much, thank you." She said this without looking at him, she couldn't bring herself to just yet. Hopefully the alcohol would give her the Dutch courage to speak with him as she had so many questions and she wanted to know about him. Just him and what he liked... but first wine, wine was a good start.

Gladly taking the filled wine glass from him, she took a rather large mouthful. Instead of being dainty and swallowing gracefully, she choked on the amount and ended up coughing, which led to wine running down her chin and some landing on the table before her. Seriously! This was getting ridiculous. She had drunk wine countless times in the past; why was it when she was around Damion did she feel like she was a buffoon and a newbie to drinking? It was so embarrassing, and what made it worse was there were no napkins to clean herself with. In fact, it was not something she had really taken notice of but there were no cleaning materials at all. How was someone supposed to eat lunch without the use of a napkin? It seemed rather uncivilized to her. Wiping her mouth with the back of her hand, she finally looked at Damion and, to no surprise to her, he was smiling. It was out of her mouth before she could stop herself:

"I'm glad I amuse you. Who doesn't have napkins at a meal? I would have thought that someone of your stature would never dress a table without them. It seems to be positively uncouth!" She was so cross and knew she looked an absolute state. With no way of fixing it, she decided to just own it and ignore him for the duration of the meal, which did look fantastic. Her stomach protested loudly and at that point Vicky realized how hungry she was.

Damion actually laughed. It was not something he ever did but, at that moment, he couldn't stop himself. Thankfully, it wasn't loud enough for Victoria to hear but it was a reaction he had no control of. She looked so poised and ready to drink her wine and then when it filled her mouth so unexpectedly he couldn't help his reaction. Of course, he had known there would be nothing to clean herself up with, but when she looked at him with sheer irritation, all he could see was how deliciously beautiful she was.

Victoria was clearly fired up and that was evident by the instant color that spread across her magnificent breasts and up her neck. He wanted to lick the trail of wine that had cascaded down her chest and was now dripping at the juncture of her crossed legs. His own arousal that had finally gone was immediately back with a vengeance. When she spoke to him about civility of dressing a table, he was thrilled. Her fire was there, she was giving him a small taste of what he wanted her to do. He knew she could, and perhaps she just needed the right incentive to do it. No one had ever described him as being uncouth so it was quite a shock. But, it was refreshing none the less that she spoke so candidly. What else could she say or would say?

Damion knew at that point that he was going to have her do something at dinner that would hopefully be just enough to have her speak to him and ask him. That is was he wanted, surprisingly...He was not agreeable to lack of control, however, the flip side of this was he was in control as he was pushing Victoria to see how far he could go. He would never hurt her but at what point did she say enough! Purposely not answering her question regarding napkins, he diverted her by reaching to a bowl and offering her some fresh cut melon (ones that were too big to put in your mouth all at once) and said,

"Why don't you start with the melon? There are plenty of things to eat here but I like to start with fruit first." All the while, he was smiling at her, just a little bit. He was unable to stop as he liked what he was seeing. He enjoyed watching her and, when she tentatively took a piece, he held his breath as she brought it to her lips. The throb of his engorged erection, it seemed, was also waiting to see what would be her response to melon in her mouth. The wait was not long. Victoria put it into her mouth and closed her lips around the length of it. She looked so beautiful and the image was not lost on him, how she would look with those lips wrapped around his cock. His heartbeat quickened as she took a bite and he watched the juice run out of the side of her mouth and followed the same trail as the wine. It was such an erotic sight to see. Again, the image in his mind was of her mouth encasing his cock and her saliva dripping out of the side and blazing a trail down her chin. It took all that he had to not clear the table with his hands and take her then and there.

Apparently, Victoria had been speaking to him but his fantasy was plaguing his mind and it was not until she touched his crossed knee that he was able to come back to the moment. Still a little dazed with the image on repeat in his head, he said,

"What now? I mean pardon? Did you need something?" He sounded out of sorts to him so he could only imagine what she must think of his disorientation.

It was hard for Vicky to not wonder what just happened? Why was he acting that way? He was always present but, for a mere moment in time there, he had definitely been somewhere else. It was the first time that she had seen any loss of utter control from him. He was definitely someone who never was this unguarded. He looked lost in thought and gorgeous doing it. She wanted to lean over and kiss his lips but the thought of him reacting badly stopped her, plus she was still reeling at this odd lunch setting they were at. It was beautiful to look at and the melon was delicious but still it was strange not having any form of napkin to use. As with the wine, the juice from the melon ran down her chest. She had given up on trying to clean herself up and just figured that she would shower after lunch. She did, however, ask Damion

"Are you not going to start with the melon, as you suggested that I did?" When he didn't react that is when she leaned over a tad and touched his knee closest to her. She knew the moment that he refocused on her, even though his answer was vague and full of his own questions. His entire body changed: while he was lost in thought, his body had become relaxed and unguarded but, as he refocused, his body became more erect, more poised, more intense.

Vicky found that she enjoyed watching him. She liked seeing his body language change depending on what was happening at that moment. To see him so relaxed in thought made her wonder what was on his mind? She desperately wanted to ask but, like everything else, she

seemed unable to do so. She had never felt so tongue tied in her life. She had quite a mouth on her and was able to be quite articulate when needed.

And let's not forget sarcasm; that was second nature to her. It was how she had grown up in her family. It was necessary to be thick skinned as the battle of wits was a daily occurrence. But this was different, everything about this was different. And, for the most part, she was enjoying the adventure, but what she was feeling for Damion was something she was unsure of. When she looked at him, she found that the ability to speak her mind vanished. Yes, she was annoyed there were no napkins or linens of any kind at this lunch and she was a sticky mess and with her being naked it was extremely uncomfortable, but Vicky hand given up on trying to be modest and instead was doing her best to enjoy the array of food sitting in front of her.

When Damion had finally come back to her (so to speak), he didn't say anything or explain what had just happened but instead reached for a slice of melon and bit it in half without any juice escaping his mouth. How did he do that, she wondered? When he finished the melon without a single drop leaving those magnificent lips, she wished there was some juice on them, just so there was a reason to lean over and lick it off. Oh my goodness, she was getting aroused. She was supposed to be mad at him, but the need to be a little naughty was there.

Damion saw the moment that Victoria became aroused. Her body was not able to hide from him, not just because she was nude but also because it was evident that she too had some kind of feelings towards him. A lovely blush replaced the fiery red that had painted her body. Yes, she was annoyed at the circumstances of their lunch; however, she was so beautiful with wine and melon juice leaving a trail down her front. And her hair was wild from her swim earlier and their time together in his playroom. He had to distract himself from her. He reacted across the table for one of the bowls full of olives and began placing food onto her plate. She needed to eat as they had used a lot of energy earlier. With that in mind, he placed olives, rolled lunch meat and some cheese slices on her plate and said firmly, "Eat, you must replenish what energy you used earlier. You may not realize it but the amount of energy used is vast and I do not want you to feel faint or ill because of lack of energy. Plus, I heard your stomach growl and, as lovely as that sound was, it is a sure tell of your hunger. "

With that, he waited for her to start eating. He was fascinated by everything she did. It was not until she put an olive into her mouth did he do the same: he would mirror her in what and when she ate. Not something he had done before but it was interesting way to eat. The difference being that when Victoria put the olive into her mouth, the juice escaped her mouth. He smiled; the fact that every time she ate something dribbled out of her mouth amused him greatly. He could see that she was becoming irritated with this but he was thoroughly enjoying the experience. Tasting the combined flavors off of her skin was going to be exceptional and then, when his tongue slid up through the inner folds of her vagina, he could imagine the taste to be intoxicating mixed with all the flavors and her own juice as the perfect pairing. Perhaps he would eat off of her? He mulled over Victoria being his plate to hold his food with her laid out and an array of food placed ever so, just for him to enjoy. Feeling her hot skin under the food, and she'd no doubt shake a little from the tremor of the unknown and her own excitement. Yes, oh yes that would be happening very soon. He planned it out in his head, first course would start on her back and he would finish with her on her front. This was such an erotic image in his mind that his breathing became hitched and his erection was yet again fighting to escape the confinement of his shorts. His plan of throwing Victoria off kilter had somewhat backfired as it would seem he too was just as off kilter, with the need to take her becoming overwhelming. He had to regain control and the only way to do this would be to remove himself from her – he need space to understand what was going on here. For goodness sake, they were just having lunch together but she unnerved him. That was not good. He was the one running this but she could put him off balance very easily. What did that say about him or his control? At once he tried to regain what little control he had. He sat up straight and said,

"Once we are done with lunch, I have some work to do and you can do as you please. The only thing I ask is, if you are going to go and lay by the pool, please put on sunscreen. It may seem cool to you now but that is because of the location of the lunch venue. Don't fooled.

We're in the Caribbean and the sun is much stronger here. And, to be honest, being sun burnt is not an enjoyable experience and will make this evening quite uncomfortable for you."

He didn't give any further explanation about their evening – that too was to be a surprise. Damion decided to finish his lunch with the air of disinterest. Which could not be further from the truth. In fact, he watched everything that Victoria did. Every time her mouth opened, he wanted it to be for his cock. He noticed as her breast rose when she grabbed something else to eat and when she moaned with satisfaction for the different tastes upon her tongue. This was the hardest meal he had ever had to endure but hopefully Victoria would not see his turmoil.

Vicky was somewhat stunned by many things throughout this odd lunch. Damion had not been with her mentally only one time during this meal and throughout the rest, he had become detached from her completely. Perhaps her inability to keep food from dribbling down her body could have been the reason. She felt like a child learning to eat for the first time and it was beyond humiliating. Again, she wished that there were napkins so at least she could hide the mess that she'd created and was currently sitting in. there was a puddle of juice that she was currently sitting in. She tried to engage him in conversation but one look at his face told her that he was not interested, so instead she focused on the food. Which was delicious, so much so that she couldn't keep the moans of pleasure from breaching her mouth. She had eaten all of this food before but for some reason this was like tasting them for the first time. Everything was so fresh and delicious – it was like there was some kind of foreplay happening in her mouth.

Chapter 21

Once lunch was finished, Damion helped Vicky to her feet and brought her around to the pool deck then once there he left her without a backwards glance. It was like a slap to her face. He had dismissed her during their meal together and how she was feeling was not great. Standing rooted to the spot where he had left her, Vicky watched him walk back into the house. She couldn't believe that he didn't say anything to her or even look at her. Suddenly remembering that she was naked, she decided to walk around to where her bikini was lying on the ground, picked it up and put in back on. The material was so flimsy that it was like being naked again but at least it gave a small sense of being clothed. Taking one last look at where Damion entered the house, Vicky dove into the pool.

She embraced the cool feeling of the water against her heated flesh, not just because of the outside temperature but because of how Damion had made her feel. She was not supposed to feel anything: this was meant to be an adventure not a study into herself or to examine her

own feelings about what was happening. Where had it gone wrong? Why was she cross with his behavior at lunch? This was his house. Technically he could act however he pleased, and with the staff, luxuries and opulence everywhere you looked, it was clear that he did just that.

Vicky couldn't help but to feel put out, but why? It shouldn't matter, right? Shaking her head, she swam to the edge of the pool, which looked out to the ocean and climbed out. She decided to take a walk so followed the stone to the lawn and continued until she reached the beach. It was further than she initially thought and by the time she reached her destination she was bone dry except for a light sheen of perspiration across her body.

Sitting down onto the white sand with a thump and an audible sigh, she all but shouted to the ocean with sheer frustration. What did she do that was so terrible for him to have basically frozen her out? Was it her inability to eat like a normal adult instead of a child? That was it, wasn't it! Or had he just lost interest in her? She was trying desperately to figure this puzzle out and all the while she was burying her feet into the sand. It was comforting to do something as normal as that.

Vicky loved the beach. Her ideal vacation involved the three s's: sun, sea and sand. Where she was at the moment allowed her to be away from the intensity of the house and the goings on there. She was not complaining, for the most part, as it was definitely new and exciting but playing with the sand like this was grounding her and was a perfect way for her to clear her head. Now she just had to decide what to do. Her options as she saw it was either to go home, which was not so appealing, or to stay and do her best to be what he wanted. First, she had to figure out what that was. The problem with all of this was that Damion was everything she was not looking for. He was beyond gorgeous, educated and cultured. Yes, he was wealthy but his money didn't matter to her. He had shown her that her body was alive under his touch, not only his touch but by others too. Just thinking about that brought goose bumps to her skin. What was in store for her tonight? Vicky had no idea but, staring out to sea, she was torn with what to do.

The clear water of the ocean was inviting her in and just as she was about to go in, a shadow covered her. When she looked up, it was the man with the hot towels. She remembered his name was Simon. What did he want? She found her voice and asked him, as politely as possible – even though he had seen her naked, she did her best to not waiver when speaking to him.

"Why are you here?" Hoping that it had not come out sounding rude, she waited for his response, all the while running the sand absently through her fingers.

Simon had been given the task to make sure that Victoria had applied sunscreen, which he knew she hadn't. This was normally Zara's job but she was indisposed at the moment therefore it fell onto him this time. Not that it was a problem, he rather enjoyed their very short experience together earlier. Now though she was dressed: well, that was a joke, she might as well not have been. With the breeze coming off of the ocean, he could see her nipples clearly though her top. And her bottoms where sticking to her like a second skin allowing the folds of her outer lips to be visible. She was beautiful and he appreciated beauty. In his mind, this was the best gig he had ever been given and, if what Damion and P. had said to be true, it would be the best career ever. Clearing his throat, he said,

"Were you not told about the strength of the sun here? Therefore, as I know you have not applied

200

sunscreen, I am to do just that." All the while, he was pouring some into his hands.

Vicky was about to stand up and protest when Simon spoke again.

"There is no point in arguing about this, it can be done easily or I can make this very uncomfortable for you. Either way, it is happing." With that, he waited a moment then before she could even respond, he began rubbing it into her shoulders. Probably with more force than he should but he was trying to make a point: she was supposed to follow directions and for all intense and purpose she didn't. Therefore, this was not meant to be pleasurable even though he was getting something out of this.

Vicky was a little, no, a lot taken aback by Simon's response and the vigor in which he was applying the said sunscreen. Her once nice, quiet moment of reflection was gone, thanks to this man, and he made no apology for why he was doing what he was doing. Quite the opposite in fact. He seemed to not only taking this very seriously but was rather enjoying administering what was now turning into punishment. Vicky had forgotten to apply sunscreen but her mind was definitely somewhere else – the decision she was trying to make was weighing heavily on her mind.

She was still a little self-conscious about why Damion had chosen her to begin with as he clearly could have any woman for himself but, if she was going to stay, which was what she desperately wanted to do then she better figure out what and how to be what he wanted. That was going to be difficult: one, she had no idea what or how to be what he wanted? And two, because she had never molded for someone EVER.

Now that the assault that Simon had been administering was finished, she looked back to him to say something but as it would seem he had vanished. Looking all around her, he was nowhere in sight. It was if the sand itself had swallowed him without leaving a trail of foot prints. How could that be? How was that even possible? Unable to answer those questions, she was resigned to the fact that many things happened here by magic. As ludicrous as that sounded in her mind, it was the only explanation she had.

Getting to her feet, Vicky initially was going to into the ocean just for a moment to calm herself while being surrounded by the ocean but something stopped her. An idea came into her head, perhaps she could ask Zara what to do. Zara obviously knew Damion much better than she did so it was the obvious choice. But how? What would she say that didn't make her sound needy or pathetic? Even though it had been mere days that she had known Damion, she was beginning to feel things, strong feelings towards him and about him. That was scary and exciting as it had been a very long time since she had any feelings towards the other sex at all.

Dusting the sand off from her legs, Vicky began walking back to the house. This time however, she didn't take the direct route, instead she found herself walking through the gardens and taking in the fragrances that permeated the very air she was breathing. The palm trees varied in their type and the colors of the flowers were incredible. Vicky didn't have a green thumb at all; in fact, she always managed to kill every type of living plant. Therefore, she decided she had a black thumb instead. It was another joke within her family. The only thing she had managed not to kill was lucky bamboo, which was extremely hardy and very difficult to kill off. That is why she had a few bamboo plants in her house for color. And apart from her, these were the only living things in her house.

But walking through the garden, Vicky was lost in the feeling of her surroundings – the cool earth under her feet and the breeze coming off the ocean were affecting her senses. She reached out to touch a particularly long leaf that looked like an elephant's ear and it was smooth to touch. This truly was paradise and she was not ready to leave. Even though Damion had a way of infuriating her. He had pushed her, as he said he would, even so she had never said no or stop. Why was the question on her mind? Did she enjoy this? Yes, was the very obvious answer but would she ever say no? Of that, she was uncertain.

Vicky made it back to the pool and, without a single thought, she dove into the refreshing cool water. It had warmed with the baking sun from the afternoon and she was very pleased about that. Not to mention the sunscreen: grudgingly, she was pleased that was on her skin too as she realized it would burn in this heat without it. It was hard to feel the heat with the ocean breeze masking it. Getting out of the pool, Vicky was determined to find Zara. She set out to do just that after grabbing a towel – it probably would not please Damion to leave a trail of water throughout his house.

Chapter 22

Damion had made it back to his office once he had watched Victoria set off towards the beach. He had seen the hurt and frustration across her face and knew she must feel as if he had ignored her during their lunch. For the most part that was correct, however, the reason was not perhaps what she might think. It had everything to do with his lack of control when he was around her. This was not acceptable. He would not allow anything or anyone to take that from him; control was how he had managed to become who is was today. Looking up from the many monitors that surrounded his compound, he found P. standing in front of him. Deciding he needed to distract himself from thinking about Victoria, he said to P.

"What do we know about Simon? What is his background? Do you think he would be an asset to you or perhaps for Recess? He was able to show no feeling at lunch. In fact, there was no reaction at all, which was quite unexpected and pleasing."

Damion leaned back into his chair further, folded his arms across his chest and waited for P. to respond. He didn't really have anyone to talk to and he trusted P. to no end. Damion valued P.'s input in somethings; not many, but in this he did as P. had a vested interest in Recess.

Plus, waiting for P. to respond was calming his turbulent mind and distracting him from thinking about Victoria. It was not long before P. responded,

"He is thirty-two, full name is Cole Simon Richardson, ex Special Forces. His military record is impressive to say the least. The actual information about what he did during his time is redacted but I have attained a full copy. He has been out of the service for two years where he was basically fucking his way around the world, literally. If he wasn't doing that he was surfing all the waves he could. He was brought to my attention about a year ago, when he settled in the west coast. I have been keeping a dossier about him since then. He lived alone, not even a house plant or animal to be seen. As far as his childhood, it was typical, nothing too exciting or different to talk about. Mother, father and one sister living in a suburb of New York. Parents are retired, father was a banker and mother a school teacher. Sister is a nurse in the city. He has not been home in at least a year. Nothing to indicate why but again easily enough to find out if you need it. As far as an asset or Recess, when I give him a task he completes it without question. He is not one to say much but when he does he has authority in his voice. I have given him menial things to do and again he doesn't question or give the impression he is above it, like I said he just gets on with it. He has the whole surfer look working for him and to be honest I believe there is much more to him than he lets on. He would be beneficial anywhere you want him to be." With that P. shifted to his other foot and leaned against the wall.

Damion had thought much the same. Simon would be good anywhere: he has the look of gentleness about him but that could be a facade for something else. He was also a good-looking enough something that Damion needed for Recess. However, thinking about where to put him was a puzzle. Damion needed someone with military knowledge for Recess but perhaps Simon would be suited to be groomed for personal detail? Damion would need to figure that out and soon. The completion of Recess was drawing near. But for now, he would keep Simon close and watch him. Then perhaps he would know what to do with him. One thing for sure, Simon would stay in Damion's employment doing something somewhere around the world.

Looking towards the monitors on his desk, Damion could see that Victoria was playing with the sand on the beach and deep in thought. That was written all over her face. What was she thinking? Was he in her thoughts? Did she want to stay? Did she want to leave him? God, he hoped not. Zooming in, he saw that her skin was pinkish which told him that she did not apply sunscreen as his request. This needed to be rectified immediately. Turning to P. Damion said,

"I will think about Simon and make my decision soon but for now I want him to go put sunscreen on Victoria." He was a little agitated by her lack of sense on this issue. If she was burnt she would be uncomfortable and by default he wouldn't be able to do what he wanted with her. He knew she was distracted after lunch but this was foolish; sunburn can quickly turn into heatstroke which is not fun at all.

"That's all for now". Damion dismissed P. with that and got back to reading his emails, of which there were many.

P. cocked his eyebrow up, gave a curt nod and left the office as quietly as he came into it. People generally gave him a wide birth, not wanting to be on the receiving end of his wrath. He ran an exceedingly tight ship and if you were not pulling your weight, you were out. Not just out of a job: depending of the infraction, you disappeared.

P. found Simon drinking water in the kitchen and said,

"Go administer sunscreen to Victoria, she is at the beach." P. was not one to mince words and he didn't repeat himself. He felt you were an adult, therefore once was enough. Having given the required instructions, he turned and left the kitchen to work on his other project.

Chapter 23

Simon was enjoying the cool, refreshing water pouring down his throat when P. came in and gave his direct order. Simon had found that P. didn't converse; he stated what he wanted then left. Simon wanted to ask why him and not Zara but P. had left the room before he had swallowed. With a satisfactory sigh, he recapped the water bottle and headed to the pool deck where the sunscreen was on the table. Once there, he grabbed it and headed to the beach.

The sun was baking overhead. And he found on the walk that he was becoming more aware of the heat against his flesh. He knew what it was like to be burned: it reminded him of a time in the desert when there was no shelter or water. The memories were not the best and now was not the time to revisit. Shaking his head, he pushed them away for now and headed off to his destination.

Simon had scoped out the entire property when he had arrived and had found that there were many passages that where hidden to the naked eye. Unless you knew what to look for, you would never see them even when they were in plain sight. This particular one led straight to the beach without being seen. It was obvious to Simon that Damion was serious about his secrecy as well as his safety. He didn't know very much about his employer but the pay was great, the job so far was easy and the location was almost perfect. The only thing missing was surf-able waves; however, on this island, the waves were gentle, having been broken by the reef a few hundred feet off the beach. It was an idyllic location with the entire property under constant surveillance.

On reaching the beach, Simon slipped up behind Victoria making sure that his shadow would be felt and visible. When she turned her head and said, "Why are you here?" he knew she was trying to be polite. For the most part, it came out that way, but her could see her involuntarily shake a little. Worry lines creased her forehead and, having studied her a little, he could tell she was deep in thought about something.

Perhaps it was to do with the lunch? It was not something he had ever witnessed and it was quite a show. At the end of the day, it was not up to him how his boss conducted himself with others. However, if for one second Simon thought that a woman was being mistreated, then he would step in but not before. That was a rule he stood by: women were the weaker sex and he would never stand by and watch anything negative happen to them.

Responding to her question, Simon stated rather than answered with,

"Were you not told about the strength of the sun here? Therefore, as I know you have not applied sunscreen, I am to do just that." The sternness was laced and undeniable in his voice, but he could see that she was getting ready to stand. Judging by the look on her face, it was clear she was about to protest. Without allowing her to speak, Simon continued,

"There is no point in arguing about this. It can be done easily or I can make this very uncomfortable for you. Either way, it is happing." He was watching her face very carefully for signs of distress. Not seeing any, he began applying the sunscreen with slightly more force than was probably necessary. He was not a mean man – he just believed in following directions to the letter. Perhaps that was because of all the years he had spent in the military; but whatever the reason, he lived his life by that. It had kept him out of trouble more times than he could count.

Not wanting to open that Pandora's Box, he brought himself back to the task at hand. Finishing with his job, he didn't wait for Victoria to say anything: he just left the way he came.

Once back to the house, he was back to finishing his water. He had been given a list of things to complete and, going down the list, he moved onto the next thing. Which was go to the far end of the island, start a perimeter search and work his way back to the main house. This would take a few hours. With that, he recycled the water bottle, grabbed another and headed outside.

Chapter 24

As much as Phillippe and Zara where both enjoying the afterglow of their afternoon delight, it was time to get back to work. The buzz from the house had come through about five minutes ago meaning they were expected back at the house with in the next twenty-five minutes. Having Zara lying naked across his body like a beautifully soft blanket made it difficult for Phillipe to want to get up. Nevertheless, it was imperative to get up.

Phillippe gently nuzzled Zara and spoke to her softly,

"*Mon amour*, as much as I am loving this, we need to get back to work." All the while, he was caressing her bare back. He loved the feel of her skin under his touch. Phillippe would never get complacent with the gift of love and devotion that Zara bestowed to him. Nor would he take what they had for granted.

Zara had slowly come awake with the gentle kisses and words from Phillippe. She was enjoying the moment, right down to the feel of his heartbeat in her ear. She frowned slightly —the last thing she wanted to do was get up and go back to work. Not that it was particularly difficult, this time, as she would have brought Victoria to climax, which she would have very much enjoyed if she had stayed. But being with Phillippe, even for a few stolen hours, was worth everything to her.

Looking up at his magnificent face, she said,

"No, I don't want to move." Yes, even to her it sounded slightly whiny.

Phillippe answered with amusement in his voice,

"We must. We will have all of next week to recapture this moment. Remember, we are going to our home and we can do anything we want – at any time. However, right now we still need to do what we are here for. Yes?"

Gently moving her from his stomach, Phillippe sat then stood up. Zara was loving watching his long, lean body move with such grace and fluidity; how he floated around a room was a thing of beauty.

"Ugh, I suppose I should get dressed, I know we are here for a reason and I know what that reason is. For the most part, I love our life. I mean there is no other occupation that would allow us to live like this..."

"But?" said Phillippe.

"But, as you said, it would still be wonderful to just stay in bed all day with you, now or whenever we wanted." She absently ran her hand over the warm spot Phillippe had just vacated. Leaning into that spot, she could smell him – he had a smell all to his own. Everyone did but, like everything else about Phillippe, she was partial to his scent. Perhaps she could entice him back to bed by rubbing herself for his pleasure. Yes, she would try. They had twenty minutes until they were needed back at the house. Surely, they could have another round of love making done within that time?

That's what they did, they made love each and every time. There was always so much passion when they were together that it was addictive with no end in sight and, as far as she could see, they both felt it. Turning onto her back and stretching, Zara began the slow process of running her hands down the sides of her body. Turning her head towards him, she brought her hands around to cup her breasts and, with the thumb and index fingers, began applying pressure to her nipples. It immediately brought a moan from her lips. With her eyes fixed on her husband, she could see that he was watching every move she was making. Teasing him some more, she brought one hand away from the breast it was cradling and moved it ever so slowly down to her bare *chatte,* as Phillippe called it.

Everything always sounded better in French and that definitely sounded better in French. With her legs spread, her fingers began a slow dance around her already hard clit and dipped lower, feeling her gathering moisture. With deliberate focus, she pushed her finger inside and immediately felt the fluid encase the digit. Pulling her finger out of her, she brought it to her lips. But, before she could make to her mouth, Phillippe grabbed her wrist and thrust the wet finger into his mouth with such suction that nothing would be left. Looking at Phillippe, she saw his eyes were on fire with desire and, taking advantage of that, she positioned herself so her legs were hanging off the side of the bed and he was nestled between them. Taking both his hands, she grasped his hips and pulled his body closer to hers. She could feel his hot erection pressing against her opening and all it would take was one pull and he would be inside her.

Phillippe knew what she was doing... he quite enjoyed the show, but they didn't have time for this right now. Tasting her from her finger only made him want her more. They did have about twenty minutes but for what he had in mind that was not nearly enough time to worship her body. He could feel her juice on the tip of his cock and there was nothing more delicious than that. But, instead of allowing her to pull him into her, he backed up and bent over to taste her bounty for himself on his tongue. With one long, deep lick, he tasted her from bottom to top and brought his tongue to her opening. He plunged as far as his tongue could go and dragged it out, curling the end to cup her arousal onto his tongue.

He could hear Zara moaning with delight but that was all she could get at the moment. With a wicked thought in his mind, he plunged again and grazed his teeth across the bundle of nerves of her hard clit and dipped his index finger into Zara's other hole. It was extremely tight but with her juices running down to it, there would be no pain, only pleasure. He heard her breath hitch and, after a couple of thrusts, he pulled out of her tight hole, brought his mouth to encase her clit and sucked as hard as he could.

Teasing with his tongue and teeth, Phillippe felt Zara began to lift her hips to meet his mouth but at that moment he let go. He pulled back. He could feel his raging erection bounce with his heartbeat but, looking at Zara, he decided to leave her the way she had found him earlier. Aroused and ready to love him the only way she knew how. She wouldn't be pleased but they had the night after dinner to themselves and the possibilities were endless.

"*Non*, that is enough for now. We will have tonight, *mon amour*. I know what you are doing but not now, we must shower and go back to the house. Yes, I know you want more and you will get it. But right now, I want you to think about how you feel right now. How it is going to intensify over the course of the day. When you are in the shower and you are washing your body and you feel your hands, think of them as not your own but mine. When you are with Victoria, think of me and what you would do for me, how you would please me." With that, he bent down, kissed her passionately and headed for the shower. He need a very cold one if he was to get through the rest of the day without having a very visible hard on.

Zara realized her plan had back fired. She had wanted to tease and torment him but instead he had turned the tables on her and she was no better off than when she had found him earlier that afternoon. He had gone for a shower and she was left lying on the bed panting with need. It took all she had not to finish of the job herself. Not that she couldn't, she could and had done so before but there was something playful about Phillippe right now and she was ready to play with him. This was not how they had done things before but she liked where it was going.

Once he was out of the shower, she stepped in and rushed through it. Even then, his words were running wild in her head. Every time she touched herself to wash, she could only see his hands touching her. Her body was on edge and it was almost impossible to not come from her own touch. Speeding through the shower, Zara got out and redressed in the white shorts and spaghetti-strapped camisole. Leaving their bedroom, she found Phillippe sitting on the couch waiting for her. She couldn't help but smile and leaned down for a quick kiss. The electric current that went through her was intense and, looking into his eyes, she saw that it was affecting him as well.

"Hmm, I like where you are going with this. I am willing to play but be careful I wouldn't want you to feel you need to do this for me. I love you and everything you are, remember that." She stood up and reached for the door knob. She felt Phillippe standing behind her and before she could say anything his hands had slipped up her camisole to cup her breasts in the same way she had on the bed, pinching her nipples and sending jolts of fire down to her groin.

Phillippe intended this to be intense, not because he thought this was what she wanted but because this is what he wanted. He had many things to show her and this was just the start. Feeling her nipples elongate with his touch, he ground his erection into her bottom and said,

"I do this because I want to, I love you also but never worry about the reason why I do things. There are many things we haven't explored together yet and we have a life time to take that journey but right now I want you to feel what my touch can do to you anytime I please. I can smell your arousal and it truly turns me on to no end. I am very much looking forward to later tonight – the question I have is, are you going to make it? We shall just have to see. Come, we must go."

Withdrawing his hands from beneath her top, he led them out of their house and down the path. Holding her hand and feeling the warmth of the late afternoon sun, he stopped and brought his hands to cradle her face and kissed her as gently as he could without any other contact. This would be a small test to see how she could respond to him in this way. As it was, he loved her unconditionally but he, like the world, wanted to evolve with her.

Zara was excited and nervous at the prospect of what would happen later. She had never seen this side of Phillippe and she was very excited by it. He had cleared up that this was not about what he thought she wanted but what he wanted instead, to do to her. That was important to her, she didn't want one-sided ever again. That was part of her past many times over but everything with Phillippe was special. The way he had made her feel just before they had left their house was adding to her want and need of him. Hopefully, the next few hours would pass quickly but she couldn't be sure about that. What she did know was the gentle kiss he had given her on the path while cupping her face had almost done her in. She was a sucker for that, and he always did that to her.

Breaking apart, they headed back to the house just in time to see P. standing on the pool deck waiting for them. Zara squeezed Phillipe's hand and walked past P. without stopping and entered the cool interior of the house.

Phillippe watched Zara walk into the house and looked at P., who was still standing in front of him. He just waited for P. to speak – it didn't take long.

He said, "Phillippe, make sure that the dining room table is the correct one for this evening's meal. You and Zara will be in attendance for the meal." Like with everyone else he left after saying what he had to say.

Before Phillippe could think of a reply, P. had left so he went into the house himself to see which table was there.

Chapter 25

Zara walked into the house with nothing on her mind but the words Phillippe had said on constant repeat. Every fiber in her body could actually feel him touching her as he had described. Just walking around had her skin coated with goose bumps. Granted, partly because Damion kept the temperature in the house lower than they kept their home on the grounds or at their primary residence, but that was only a fraction of why she was so hyper sensitive.

After having walked into the kitchen, where she saw the chef who was preparing dinner for Damion and Victoria, she left there and went in search of Damion. She needed know what this evening would entail, and therefore giving her an idea of what clothing needed to be laid out for Victoria, if any.

She found him in his office feverishly typing something – probably an email to someone overseas. She smiled at her silly mistake; of course, it would be to someone overseas as they themselves were out of the United States. Mentally shaking her head, she tried to compose herself. She was so out of sorts with naughty thoughts put there by Phillippe that she was having a hard time focusing on what she was to do next.

She watched Damion for a few minutes in silence. She was really looking at him, not as her boss or what he was before they agreed to this new arrangement but really looking at him.

Taking in the way his hair lay, the angles of his face, she realized that he was a perfect man. They should make marble casts of him and have them displayed over the world to admire his sheer beauty. She was not in love with him but she was not blind either and she appreciated his raw rugged maleness. Casting her eyes lower, she couldn't see his chest or torso but from memory knew it was tight and muscular. Like everything in his life, he controlled how he looked and this was done by a strict regime of exercise daily.

Damion was too much for Zara but he was an excellent boss. Working for him had many perks. One was the ability to travel and see things most people would never see. Nor anyone from her home town. That, was not much to talk about and definitely not somewhere that Zara wanted to bring her husband. Phillippe wanted to visit her hometown but she was doing everything in her power to not go back. She had left for a reason and had no reason to return, too many memories, wounds that had not healed and, to be honest, she was not sure they ever could heal.

Hearing Damion sigh, she looked at his face; he was watching her. He was very good at reading people and hiding things from him rarely worked. Zara simply said,

"What are the plans for dinner? Which outfit would you like Victoria to be in?"

She sounded a little rushed and breathless. Hopefully, she had hidden it well but judging by the look on Damion's face, it clearly had not gone unnoticed.

Damion let the smile climb around his mouth, knowing that Zara had not be fulfilled and was balancing on the precipice of pleasure. He knew that she had gone to Phillippe and had assumed he had sated her, but it was clear that Phillippe had left her wanting more. Phillippe had surprised him and that was not easily done. He was climbing in Damion's estimation. Damion thought he had known what Zara needed but when Phillippe had come to him all that had changed.

Damion was questioning himself with regards to Victoria and dinner, what did he want her in? He rather enjoyed lunch with her completely nude for him to gaze at but would that be too much for dinner? He had had custom clothes made for Victoria and it would be a waste and a shame to not see her model them for him. Yes, she would be clothed tonight. With that in mind, he said to Zara,

"The plans are that dinner shall be in the dining room with the table set for formal dinner. You and Phillippe shall be there in attendance against the wall to observe. I want her in the teal dress with shoes of your choosing. As usual, she is to be bathed and pampered to my standards. I am sure that today she will be needing it more than yesterday. I know she will be in your capable hands so be even more attentive please. That's all, I shall see you in the dining room at seven." With that said he re-focused on his monitor that was in front of him and continued typing.

Clearly, Zara had been dismissed. Not in the least bit upset by his way of being done with her, Zara left the office in search for Victoria.

Chapter 26

As it was, Victoria was in the bath in the bedroom she had been assigned to when she arrived here. There were no soaps or shampoos but sometimes all you needed was a good soak in hot water to ease any nerves or ailments that one might have.

Zara stood in the doorway watching Victoria. She had her head resting against the tub with her eyes closed, all that could been seen above the water was her slender neck and head. She had pulled her hair so it was draped over the edge and her hands were idly playing with the water creating ripples. With each breath she took, her nipples broke the surface and water droplets would race down her breasts with speed, vying to see which one would win. Her eyes were closed so Zara was as quiet as she could be; she had already laid out the dress Victoria was to wear – of course there was no underwear to be put on – and her shoes were ready for her. Zara had brought with her the soap and shampoos she would need to wash Victoria; she could lounge in the bath for a few more minutes but she would be getting into the shower for the actual cleaning. Unlike the time in the bathing room, Phillipe would not be joining them. After Damion had said that she might be needing more attention, Zara thought it would be best if she was not distracted by her husband and could solely focus on Victoria. Playing Phillippe's words around Zara's head she couldn't help but feel the arousal begin to build. She needed to tamper that down if she was to do her job properly, her focus was to be on Victoria by making her feel: what she was to feel was yet to be seen?

Walking into the bathroom, Zara cleared her throat and said,

"Good evening, Victoria."

Before she could say anything else, Victoria said,

"Oh, hi. I'm really glad you are here. I have a few questions to ask and you're the only person I could possibly ask."

Vicky leaned to the left and brought her body to the side of the bath. It was warm and she was able to cover herself just a little, even if it was just for a few minutes while she asked the very important question.

Zara was not expecting that. Yes, Victoria had seemed deep in thought but Zara had thought that she was just relaxing. However, that did not seem to be the case. Hesitantly, she said

"Okay, you may ask me anything but I don't have to answer you. Is that fair? Remember, I don't want to lose my position here. What is your question?"

Gathering all of her courage, Vicky said,

"Okay, I understand. However, it's not just one question and I hope you do answer because otherwise I don't know what I'm going to do. So, my first one I have been thinking all afternoon. What I could possibly have done wrong with Damion? I'm unable to think of anything, other than my inability to eat like and adult; which I might add was totally embarrassing! Is that he just is not into me in the way I hope he would be? I know, I know... that sounds totally desperate and pathetic, but hear me out. I'm in this situation – which is kind of weird by the way – and yes, I agreed to it, but it is still odd. I've never ever heard of anything like this happening to anyone I know. But, in saying that, I'm trying very hard to embrace all the new and kind of exciting things that have happened so far. Now don't get me wrong, Damion has infuriated me beyond belief and I would love to yell at him but the truth is I don't want to disappoint him." Sighing and swirling the water around her, she continued,

"He could have any woman he wanted, so I do feel I'm the lucky one here. For now. But that's part of my problem."

"What is?" asked Zara.

"I don't know what he wants! He asked me once to tell him what I wanted but I couldn't bring myself to utter the words. What if that was test and I failed him? What do I do? How can I be what he wants if he doesn't talk to me? I think, no I'm sure, I have feelings for him. What feelings, I have no idea so I'd like to figure them out but not if he doesn't want me here. So Zara, my question is: how can I be what Damion wants?

Please, I'll take anything you have to give me. Don't think I'm a desperate woman, I was very happy in my little world on my own but Damion has made me feel something I have never before and I'm not ready to give that up, unless it would be for the best. What do you think?"

Feeling more exposed than when she was naked, Vicky waited for what seemed like an hour for Zara to respond. Not only had she opened up to (for all intense and purposes) a total stranger but her heart was racing. She just hoped, no wished, for some kind of insight to Damion and, let's be honest, who would be better than

Zara to give her that? Well, not better but she had no idea whom else to ask. Vicky felt that there was something more to the relationship between her and Damion but she had no idea what. Right now though, she just wanted help being more of what he wanted.

Zara looked at Victoria in the bath gazing up at her with such yearning for the answers to her questions. The problem was there was no easy answer. Damion was a very complex man. He did things the way he did them for a reason; however, having Victoria here was not the norm and it not only had thrown his staff off, but it was clear that he too was unsure. It was obvious to Zara that Damion had feelings towards Victoria too but it was not her place to say anything. This was going to be quite difficult as not only could he see everything but there was audio as well all over the compound.

Gathering her thoughts, she decided on saying,

"Mr. Foster asked you to come here for a reason. I'm not aware why but what I can say to you is that he doesn't do anything without thoroughly thinking every angle through. You don't have to be anything but yourself as that's all he's really looking for. It's what brought you to his attention in the first place.

Now, you need to get into the shower so I can wash your hair and get you ready for tonight. But get up slowly as I can see steam coming off the water. You might become lightheaded and I wouldn't want you to faint." Zara said the last bit with a smile to lighten the rather tense mood. Hopefully she had answered the questions that Victoria wanted without saying too much; only time would tell.

After walking over to the bathtub, Zara leaned down and lifted the leaver to drain the water. As she did so, she brushed her hand between Victoria's legs and heard her intake her breath. Not wanting to startle her any further, Zara removed her hand with gentleness and ease. She walked around to the head of the bath and across to the shower. She turned it on to a cooler temperature as the bath was quite hot and the cooler water would be refreshing after such temperatures. Zara would turn up the heat once Victoria became accustomed to it, therefore minimizing the possibility for her to become lightheaded.

Walking back to the bath, she waited for Victoria to get out. Zara was ready to catch her if need be, but as it was Zara didn't need to as Victoria walked straight to the shower and got in.

Vicky was at first a little put out by the evasive answer that Zara gave but, the more she thought about it, Zara was right. Damion had asked Victoria to go with him on this crazy adventure, and he did seem like the kind of man who thought everything through rather than just doing something without thinking about the consequences. She resigned herself to just being her, being what she was and if that wasn't enough then to hell with him. The one thing she needed to do was find her tongue when they were in each other's company, then maybe that would be better for them both. She would say what she wanted and in turn it might please him, as he had asked her to tell him what she wanted. Or perhaps it would backfire and she would be sent packing, either way it seemed to be the only way. She was startled when she felt Zara's hand between her legs but, as soon as she looked down, it was clear all she was doing was emptying the bath. Within a few minutes, Vicky heard the shower running and not wanting to faint, as that would just be another embarrassment, she took some time getting out the bath. In such deep thought, she didn't even think about her nakedness as she walked into the shower, nor did it register what Zara had said about washing her hair and getting her ready for tonight. When she stood under the cool spray of the shower and felt hands run down her back, she jumped! In doing so, she slipped on the tile and fell.

It felt as if she was falling in slow motion. She landed with a thump and, as her hand landed on the tile floor, a sharp slap sound reverberated around the shower stall.

Drawing her knees to her chest, she curled up into the smallest shape she could make and began to cry softly. She was not crying because she was in pain but rather because she was embarrassed: embarrassed at falling in the shower, embarrassed with her inability to eat and drink like an adult, embarrassed with all the mistakes she had made up to this point...

She was feeling really low and defeatist and thought she might hide in the shower forever. Yes, that was a tad drastic but, right know, it felt right. Her feelings were all over the place. She wanted to do better and be more of what Damion wanted, she was enjoying this experience so far and wanted to continue with it. She had been brought to such sexual highs and according to Damion this was only the beginning. What did that mean? How much higher could it get? What else could they do that would be able to take them there? It was all just overwhelming her right now, right here in sitting on the shower floor. Knowing that Zara was there didn't help her embarrassment, it just intensified the feeling. What did feel really good right now was the water cascading over her, the waterfall effect was just that; effective.

Vicky felt arms close around her and felt her body being drawn back into Zara's embrace. This just felt right and she leaned into the other woman, feeling the comfort that was being given to her. They stayed like that for what seemed like an hour but perhaps was only about five minutes, until Zara softly spoke, "You put too much into this. You need to just relax, allow the water to wash away any ill feelings you have. You are completely safe and I am sure your body is experiencing things for the first time; this is normal. It is normal to be overwhelmed. I know lots of this is new to you and, if you don't mind me, saying you are handling this very well. Not many women could or have done this well: that should make you feel a bit better about this whole thing, no?"

"Yes, it does; well, it kind of does." Thinking about what Zara just said, Victoria wondered did that mean others had done this as well? What did that mean? Pulling away from Zara perplexed, she asked,

"What did you mean by "other women did not handle this well"? Have there been many before me? Oh my God, what is this place? Is that why I'm not able to just walk around the house on my own? Are there other women being held here? Am I going to be held here against my will? Are you being held against your will?"

Vicky was becoming frightened, what the hell was happening here? Nothing was making any sense, she had to get up and get some distance from Zara. Standing, she walked to the wall behind the spray and crossed her arms against her stomach, waiting for an explanation but judging by previous conversations she was not hopeful. She was looking at Zara and Zara was smiling, why was she smiling? Was she brainwashed? Vicky was so confused.

Steadying her breathing, she asked again, "Please, can you just give me a straight answer. What is this place? Who is Damion? Is he involved in some kind of human trafficking?" As she waited, she ran her hands over her and down her hair, then back to a resting place across her stomach.

Zara swore to herself. She should never had let that slip. If Damion had heard, he would be irate. She had to fix this! Victoria had clearly let her mind run wild in thinking that this was some sort of place to condition women for trafficking. Just thinking about what Damion would say sent shivers down her spine, and not in a good way. As gently and firmly as possible, Zara said, "No, it's not what you are thinking Mr. Forster is not involved in human trafficking. This is one of his private homes. I'm not, nor have I ever been, held against my will. No one here is or will be. Like you, we are free to leave whenever we want. As it is, I particularly like my employment here, along with everyone else. Otherwise, we would not be here at all.

As far as other women, I should not have said anything. What I can say is that you are the first to be here by Mr. Forster's request and the first at this location. He is a man and a very handsome one at that so you must see that having women sexually or otherwise is not outlandish. Like most men, he has a varices appetite for such things but you need not worry. You are completely safe here: no harm will come to you at all and nor to anyone else. Come, we must hurry now and get you ready for tonight, I promise you are no way in any sort of danger. Remember

228

when we first met and I said you could trust me? Well, that's still the case."

Waiting to gauge Victoria's reaction and hoping she had fixed her *faux pas,* she moved towards her and pulled her until she was under the jets entirely.

Vicky surprisingly was eased with the explanation that Zara had given and quite astounded that she had been give straight answers opposed to the run around she felt she had gotten since arriving. Her imagination was running away with her and to be honest she really didn't think Damion would be involved in such an awful endeavor. He seemed to be far too refined for that sort of thing. As it was, she had no idea what he did but right now it was of no consequence. What she did know was that for some reason that she couldn't explain, she did feel safe here, with Zara but also here at this house. She was absolutely confused about Damion but she didn't feel unsafe around him. She actually felt the opposite, which was good considering the alternative. With that in mind, she allowed Zara to pull her under the spray; Zara had turned up the heat a little and it was helping her calm down. Walking forward towards Zara, she said, "I'm sorry. Sometimes my mind takes a journey all of its own and my imagination works overtime. I guess that's why I write: so they leave my head and are on paper instead, or rather my computer. Funny though, I haven't even thought about writing since I have been here, wonder why? Huh." Again, she ran her hands down her hair and turned so that Zara could start washing it. She had just accepted that this was the way it was. Zara bathed her and she did nothing but enjoy the process. Wondering a little what it would be like to go back to her normal un-interesting life was not so fun but in less than a week it would be a reality. But right now, this was her reality so she intended to enjoy it.

Watching Victoria visibly relax was a good thing. Zara let out the breath she had been holding and really hoped that this conversation would never come back to haunt her. Damion would not be pleased but Zara had diffused the situation well for now anyway. She had managed to avoid explaining about the others and why they were here or how they left. The bell had not been talked about and she certainly was not the one to bring it up.

Victoria had mentioned her writing. Zara did not want to question that so she let it go but she would let Damion know that part of their conversation. There were only two places in this house where there was no sound: all the showers and Damion's quarters. You could hear if someone was shouting but not a conversation inside the shower so there was hope he would never hear about this at all.

When Victoria turned her body around, Zara started washing her hair thoroughly, making sure to condition it well. Tonight, Victoria needed to feel extremely relaxed. Zara didn't know what was in store but she did know that she was to be in attendance along with Phillippe. Washing her back, she felt that Victoria's muscles were very tight. She would need to pay extra attention while applying lotion so she could ease those muscles. Making quick but careful use of the shower, she finished washing Victoria in record time and brought her out and dried her off. There was a handy button at the entrance of the shower that would switch off one of the nifty things that were in this house.

Vicky willingly followed Zara into the bedroom, where she knew that lotion would be applied then she would be dressed. What in, she had no idea, but if she had to guess it would be gorgeous just like everything else she had worn since arriving here.

Zara took great care while applying the lotion and indeed did take special care in massaging her shoulders and back.

"Lie down on the bed and I will rub the tension from you." Zara said.

Knowing that the shower was not in the least bit sensual, Zara knew she had to do something to bring Victoria to the point before dinner, but how would be challenging. Rubbing lotion in could be an easy way to do it though.

Vicky was happy to oblige. She loved nothing more than getting massages and went at least once a week at home so having one here would be great. And she was tense; she didn't realize it until Zara brought it to her attention. She walked to the bed and lay down face first letting her body sink into the sumptuous bed. She felt the bed dip as Zara climbed up and straddled her bottom. She felt the weight of her there but was oddly comforted by this. She braced herself for the cold lotion dripping on her back but was pleasantly surprised when it didn't come. Rather Zara must have poured some into her hands and warmed them up. When her fingers made contact with her skin, Victoria just melted under the pressure. All her tension vanished and she was very content, so much so that she sighed and said, "Oh, so good!"

Zara smiled knowing that what she was doing was indeed working. She worked on the tense areas then carefully moved lower across her bottom and down her legs. Pulling them apart she worked up the inside and back down again. She was indeed bringing her hands closer to her pussy, but not yet! Victoria was not ready for that. She probably would jump like a scalded cat and that was definitely not the desired reaction.

Instead, Zara took her time. carefully and with purpose, she inched her fingers closer and closer until she was finally brushing the outer smooth lips and moving away again. Only to bring them back again with a little more exploration to brush her lips and run up the opened slit.

Unconsciously, Victoria had opened her legs further, allowing her lips to fall naturally and giving Zara permission to continue with her massage. It was too tempting to not delve into the creamy center, so she did, and the cream coated her index finger. Pushing deeper she felt Victoria's walls clamp around her and heard her breath quicken.

Zara knew not to go too far with this as Victoria could come apart at any moment. Instead, she chose with draw and drag her soaked finger down across the hard bundle of nerves of her clit. She pushed against it and removed her fingers. For her own sanity, she had to!

She heard Phillippe's words in her head, reminding her that this was what he was doing to her and if she was not careful she too would come apart. She was never allowed to do that with one of the playmates and, as Damion had not given her permission, she wouldn't do it with Victoria either. Refocusing on the massage, she worked the lotion over Victoria's arms and said, "Turn over please." Vicky gladly obliged. She had given over to whatever came her way. She was floating on this wonderful feeling and didn't want it to end anytime soon. Turning over, she was rewarded with Zara's deftly hands dancing along her body and bringing lightning trails with them. Without looking, she knew her nipples had pebbled and, had it not been today, she would have covered herself up, but her body betrayed her and she couldn't move. She was somewhere between the build of an orgasm and absolute relaxation: was that even possible? She didn't care right now, that was for later to think about. What she did know, emphatically, was that she needed to feel Damion touch her body again. This was great with Zara but she needed him, wanted him, and had to have him. Her skin began changing color thinking about Damion doing this to her instead of Zara and she could feel her juices abscond her core. Without thinking, one word escaped her lips,

"Damion...!" she said with a purr.

Zara heard Victoria and knew she was ready, she was in a very pliable state. Zara removed herself from the bed and walked over to the closet, opened it and pulled out the dress she was to put Victoria in. The teal dress was in the Grecian style. It was made entirely of chiffon and reached mid-thigh in length. Zara left it hanging on the door of the closet.

Walking back to the bed, Zara gently pulled Victoria up to a sitting position. She could see that Victoria's skin was blush pink. She looked beautiful and, with this dress, she would be everything Damion could ever want in a woman. Victoria was proving to be more than what Zara had initially thought.

Bringing Victoria to a stand, she brought her away from the bed and over to the vanity to dry her hair. Once that was done, Zara walked over to the closet, grabbed the dress and brought it to Victoria.

Vicky watched Zara come back from the closet with the most beautiful dress she had ever seen, even more so than the one from the night before. This was teal and had layers upon layers of chiffon. It looked to be rather short but it didn't matter, she couldn't wait to put it on. Looking around for underwear, she didn't find any and looked back at Zara saying, "That is gorgeous, but I don't see any underwear. Surely, I'm not expected to wear this without any? Am I?"

"Yes, you are. This dress is beautiful but not as beautiful as you. You don't need underwear; you are perfectly covered with this dress. I have chosen silver sandals for your feet. You will look like the Grecian Goddess that you are."

Zara could not keep the smile from her face. With this dress Damion would not know what to do. Victoria would take his breath away.

"Come, let get you dressed."

With that, Zara pulled Victoria up and had her step into the dress, pulling it up past her hips, lifting her left hand to thread it through the only strap that would drape across her entire shoulder. The front would lie diagonally across her breasts and taper into the waist, allowing the skirt to flow around her thighs. The whole dress would sit loosely on Victoria's body but hug in all the right places.

Glancing at the mirror, Vicky saw how beautiful she really was in this dress. Zara was right. It was still weird, not wearing underwear, but now she could see that she didn't need it.

What she didn't notice was that the dress pulled across her breasts exposing her areola and nipples and when she walked the chiffon was not a thick as she might think: her bottom and her pubis would be visible.

She looked like a Goddess of the Sea: she didn't need any makeup. The only thing Zara did was put on the sandals and gather her hair into a high ponytail leaving a few strands to frame her face.

Very pleased with her work, Zara stood back and said,

"Right, let's get you to dinner. I have no idea what's on the menu but no doubt it will be fantastic!"

"Oh, okay. I'm not really hungry so I hope it's not too much of a meal. But I am sure it will be delicious as everything here is." Smiling and feeling very pretty, Vicky followed Zara out of the bed room and down into the dining room.

Chapter 27

Damion was anxiously waiting for Zara to bring Victoria down for dinner. Victoria had been flustered and annoyed when he had last seen her. Granted, he had made her that way. Hopefully though, with Zara's influence, she would be in a happier mood or rather in a different mood.

Phillippe was standing against the wall behind him as he had been instructed. He wasn't saying anything to Damion, but that was okay with him as all he could focus on was waiting to see Victoria in the dress he had chosen for her. It had seemed like an eternity waiting for them. Strangely, when they walked in and Damion saw Victoria, butterflies beat wildly in his stomach. What was that he wondered?

She was every bit the vision he knew she would be in that dress. If he wasn't such a possessive man, he would have paraded her around for all to see. However, he was possessive and he just couldn't, not yet. He wanted her, all of her for himself right now.

Watching her walk into the room took his breath away, and watching the chiffon fabric strain across her chest made him jealous of the clothing. He wanted to be touching her, holding her. As crazy as it sounded, he was jealous of the fabric! This made him smile; that was definitely new and odd.

The sun that had touched her this afternoon had brought some depth to her porcelain skin, the bronzing just enough to brighten her skin tone. Fortunately, she was not burnt. That was something he had been annoyed about earlier but he was pleased Simon had taken care of that.

Unable to stop himself, he got up from his seat and walked to her as slowly as his impatient body would allow. She stood just inside of the dining room; her fingers were fidgeting with the helm of the dress. Lucky for her (and him), it was mid-thigh so she didn't have to stretch; however, every time she pulled it taught, he was rewarded with the view of her pubis. It took every ounce of his strength to not cup her sex and feel it in his hand. Instead, he walked to her and said, "Victoria, you are beautiful. Please give me the honor of your company for dinner. I assure you, you will enjoy it."

He waited for her answer. Outwardly, he was calm but inside he was doing everything in his power to remain the façade of in control.

When Vicky had walked into the dining room, she didn't need to search for Damion. He was sitting at the head of the table looking as relaxed as one could be. At that moment, all she could see was the shirt he was wearing. He had on a white fitted dress T-shirt that accentuated his magnificent tan, his hair was damp from what she assumed was a shower and when he stood up she saw that he was wearing khaki wheat-colored trousers and brown flip-flops. He was a God all to himself. When he walked towards her, he did so slowly and never took his eyes off of hers. She was a little nervous and was playing with the helm of the dress she had on. He didn't touch her but he did ask her to join him for dinner and it would be rude not to so she answered. "Yes, I would like that very much, what are we having?"

"Does it matter?" he answered, hoping she would respond honestly. To his astonishment, she did.

"Well, you see, I'm not really hungry. So, as much as I'm loving the food, I just hope it's not too heavy." Proud that she had said what was on her mind, she held her breath, waiting for him to say something. It didn't take long until he did.

"Lucky for you, dinner is light tonight; we're having fish and some vegetables. Will that be enough? If not, I have a dessert in mind for after dinner." That he said with a wink and a generous smile. He knew she would get the innuendo: perhaps that would be enough to forgive his behavior at lunch.

Vicky was pleased that Damion seemed to be in a very playful mood, unlike the distant one at lunch. This dinner was looking up and, judging by his response, perhaps they would have dessert after all. That was certainly something to look forward to.

"Yes, that is fine." Feeling a little playful, she added.

"Can you tell me what flavor dessert will be?" she hoped he would play.

As it was, he did.

"Let's just say that vanilla is most definitely not on the menu. I do, however, have many other flavors you can try. But first, let's eat." With that he walked Victoria to her seat next to his instead of at the other end of the table.

Vicky had been solely focused on Damion so she had not noticed Zara join Phillippe against the wall behind Damion's seat. That seemed a little strange, or maybe they were to help with the dinner service. Taking her seat, she reached over for the water glass and took a very cautious sip. She did not want to spill anything tonight. She was pleased when not a single drop slid down her chin. Smiling, she put the glass back and sat back, a little more relaxed, and waited; for what, she was not sure but just being next to Damion was good enough right now.

Damion, on the other hand, had been toying with an idea, whether he was going to go through with it had not been undecided until now. Clearly Victoria was in a playful mood, therefore he would up their game drastically.

He watched her take a tentative sip of water and saw how pleased she was that she had managed to not spill anything. She visibly relaxed and sat back leaning against the back of the chair. With the skirt pulled under her, she was entirely exposed for Damion to feast his eyes on. The only thing better would be her lying naked under him – hopefully that would come as soon as dinner was finished. But for now, he needed to implement his plan. He reached to the shelf under the table and pulled up a wooden box. Watching how interested she had become in the box, he let it sit in front of him for a short while as he watched her. When he thought she was about to ask about it, he said,

"You like my box? I prefer what is inside of my box, would you like to know?" Interested, but having no idea at all what could possibly be inside, Victoria said, "Sure."

Damion sat there for a while and just watched Victoria. After a short time, when she began nibbling on her lower lip, he lifted the lid of the ornate box.

When Damion had lifted the lid of the box, Vicky could see that sitting on blue-purple velvet was a stainless-steel, egg-shaped object that was about the size of a golf ball with what looked like a matching USB lying next to it. What it was for, she had no idea at all.

Damion was enjoying this – she clearly had no idea what the contents of the box were for. Instead of telling her, he very casually said,

"I am going to hand you it and I want you to place it into your pussy: right here, right now." With that, he sat back waiting for her to respond. He expected her to be shocked; in fact, he wanted her to get verbose with him. He waited and waited until she said, "What, are you mad? I can't do this" Vicky was frantically looking around.

Damion, still very casual, said "Yes, you can, and you will. It's what I want and you agreed to be with me and do what I wanted for seven days. As far as I can tell, a week has not passed as yet. So I'm unsure why you are even questioning it." All this was said with a calm voice.

Vicky couldn't do that, there was no way that was going to happen. This was not how she thought dinner would go. She hadn't even had a chance to eat yet. She was so looking forward to dessert but there was no way that would happen now. At a total loss at what to do, she did the only thing that made any sense at that moment and she cried,

"I can't, I have to go." With that, she fled the dining room, ran down the hall, past the round table with the antique bell under its glass dome, and out of the front door.

There she found Simon, polishing the car she had arrived in. Without a backwards glance, she ran to the car, opened the back-passenger door and said to Simon, "Take me home."

She was completely broken. It had taken all of her courage to go along on this journey with Damion and, right when she thought they were about to have a normal dinner and play like a new couple would, he had asked her to do that!

Simon had heard the front door slam against the side of the house and saw Victoria run out. He had not stopped what he was doing, as he was doing a job after all, but she clearly was in distress. With tears running down her cheeks, she had asked him to take her home. Something was not right and her safety was clearly the most important issue. She had asked him to take her home so that is what he would do. He would text P. from the car to let him know where they were and what he was doing.

Getting into the driver's seat, Simon started the engine and headed towards the airstrip on the other side of the island.

In the dining room, Damion heard Phillippe say loudly

"*Mon Dieu,* are you going to let her run away?"

What had he just done? Damion was totally confused – he thought they were being playful, why had she fled? He didn't understand at all and why was Phillippe saying that to him?

"What did I do?" Damion genuinely asked Phillippe, but it was Zara that answered him.

"You pushed too hard, she was looking to please you. She would not be pleased with me telling you but I will: she wanted to be what you wanted.

Remember; she is not like the others. She is not educated in your likes and wants. She is special and, to be totally honest, she has feelings for you. I know you have feelings for her as well or you wouldn't have pushed her that far. But that was too much, too soon. You best go and get her."

Zara stood with her hands on her hips and shook her head at Damion. She was seriously pissed at him. He had done that to Victoria that on purpose, she was pretty sure, but that was not the reaction he thought she would have. But really, there was not going to be a good outcome of that.

Phillippe brought his arm around Zara and said, "Damion, you must go to her, I know you don't want to feel for her but, like you said months ago, there is something special about her and you have something with her. Go now, I am sure I heard the car pull out of the driveway." With that said, he kissed the top of Zara's head and took her out of the room to their private quarters. Damion had to figure this out for himself.

Damion walked towards the front of the house, only to be stopped by P. who said, "Simon just texted letting me know they were headed towards the airstrip. What the hell is going on?" it was unusual for P. to raise his voice.

Damion didn't even bother answering. He just said, "Take me to the airstrip."

He was foolish. He had wanted to play with her but forgot just how innocent she really was. It was a stupid mistake and, in the grand scheme, really was not that big of a deal: all she had to have said was no. But she didn't. Instead, she left, run for the hills, and that bothered him a lot. He had to talk to her make her understand what the egg-shaped object was and what it was for, then she would see reason and come back. They could continue their evening and enjoy their dinner, perhaps even take a walk around the grounds and, if she was up to it, have the dessert they had talked about. But first, he had to get to her before she took off. P. sped down the gravel driveway towards the airstrip and Damion looked out of the window, formulating a plan.

Vicky was still crying silent tears when they pulled up to the airstrip. Once they were through the guard rail, Simon drove to the hanger where the plane had been brought out. The pilot had fired up the engines but, before letting Vicky out of the car, Simon turned to her and said,

"Are you hurt?"

He was very serious about this. If for one second he thought anyone had hurt her, he would take care of the situation the only way the military taught him too.

"No, I'm not hurt, I just want to go home, please..." She was pleading with him and her arms where wrapped protectively around her waist.

Simon got out of the car and opened her door; once out, he wrapped a blanket around her body and walked her to the steps of the plane. As soon as she got to the second step, Simon heard another car pull up and stop.

She couldn't help herself from looking over her shoulder; she saw him. Damion's car door was open, he was out of the car and now had his hands-on top of it. He was staring at her with something written on his face, but what? At that moment, she didn't know what to do. Would she go home like she said she wanted to, or would she stay and see why he had followed her here?

Made in USA - Kendallville, IN
32745_9780692961520
12.15.2021 1851